That'll Do

White Wagon Books

Other Works by Kathy Wagenknecht

Away to Me

Come Bye

That'll Do

Kathy Wagenknecht

That'll Do is a work of fiction. Names, places, and incidents are products of the author's imagination or are used fictitiously

Published by White Wagon Books

ISBN-13: **978-0692298015**
ISBN-10: **0692298010**

Cover painting: Pat White

Printed in the United States of America by CreateSpace

For

Tracy, who found Our Guy

and

Linda and the MADog Gang, who addicted me to Agility

Special thanks to Ann, Betty, Jane, and Susan
Proofing Pals, Editors, and Advisors

Chapter 1 — February 15

It was the dream that did it. The one of me sitting in the corner of the kitchen peeling potatoes. I couldn't get past it.

I dithered for another day before calling back my old college roommate, Barb King, with a reply. "Why not?"

"Oh, thank God, Ruth," she said. "I just can't 'widow' any more. I am exhausted by my grief and everyone's reaction to it."

"I understand. I can't peel any more potatoes," I sighed.

"Whatever do you mean?"

"You know, the old aunt sitting in the corner, peeling potatoes, while life happens around her. She becomes just another kitchen fixture until she fades totally away." I finished with a sigh.

"Is it that bad? I know your niece got married and her husband moved into the house."

"No, it's not that bad. It's not bad at all. But it could be." I sighed again.

Barb laughed. "God, Ruth, we're pitiful. I have *got* to stop this and do something different. But are you sure you're ready to leave Oklahoma?"

"Why not?" I repeated. "I want to be the one starring in my future, not fading out of it. And I hate to peel potatoes."

Chapter 2 — May 10

The day the storage Pod arrived, it was snowing. In Vermont. In May. Neighbors' heads poked out open doorways or from behind twitching curtains to watch the erector-set-inspired truck deliver the Pod. The driver expertly positioned the flatbed trailer carrying the storage unit onto the spot Barb had indicated. He lowered the frame, winched the Pod into the air, moved the truck from under the frame, and lowered the Pod into place. Magic. I had seen it first in Oklahoma three weeks earlier, but it was still an amazement.

The neighbors gradually came outside to see better. They came up singly and in groups, introducing themselves, welcoming us to the neighborhood, and asking about the Pod.

Barb and I nodded and smiled. Yes, it had all my clothing and some furniture. No, it wasn't very expensive. Yes, we would keep it for a few days while we unpacked. No, Barb's stuff would come separately.

"So, Ruth, how do you expect to fill up that big house with the piddly little bit you can fit in that Pod?" asked one sixty-something woman.

"Oh, most of the furniture came with the house," I responded. "So we really didn't have to bring much to be able to live here."

After everyone finished marveling about the technology of the Pod delivery system, we turned and walked slowly into our nearly 200-year-old house in the middle of our first Vermont snowstorm.

We had found the house online. Rather like internet dating. In fact, I am convinced that I could make a fortune with a HouseMatch.com business that would allow you to specify all the attributes of your perfect house that it would then match to the houses on file and send you the address of your dream house.

Except it didn't work that way for us. We weren't even sure where we wanted to live. We just knew it was somewhere small-ish but with enough services to be a town (I was sick of a two-hour drive to a decent grocery store), and Barb wanted some-where uncongested so that she would never again sit in traffic as she did in her native St. Louis.

We thought we would like to be close to some family, which contradicts my leaving my niece in Oklahoma, but who says we have to be consistent? Barb's upstate New York cousin, Marcy, is a realtor wannabe who took on the search with a vengeance. She daily swamped our emails with listings from real-tor.com, trulia.com, and zillow.com from upstate New York, Northwest Massachusetts, and Western Vermont.

None of her selections lit me up until she sent one titled, "An Interesting Idea." It was a listing for a "dual living house" in the historic district of Centerbury, Vermont. Initially, I dismissed it. Barb and I had never discussed anything but shared space, like we'd had in college. But the more I thought about it, the more enamored I became with the idea of two separate houses con-nected by a common cellar that could afford both privacy and companionship.

I convinced Barb that it was worth considering even though she was still stuck with the idea of love beads in the doorways like we had in 1973. She eventually commissioned her cousin to go look at the house and send us photos.

After that, every other house paled in comparison. We final-ly agreed to go see it ourselves. We spoke with the realtor and bought our plane tickets to Albany, NY, the closest airport to Centerbury.

Three days before we were to leave, we got a call from the realtor. The owners had lowered the price and there were four offers on the table. If we wanted to bid on it, we had to do it within 24 hours. Barb and I agonized about asking the house to marry us before we had seen it, but we finally jumped in, proposed, and waited to hear from the matchmaker.

Just after we arrived in Albany, the realtor called. The owners said, "Yes." We needed to plan our "wedding."

This metaphor needs elastic I am stretching it so far, but you get the idea. Forces beyond us seemed to be arranging our destiny.

To keep myself calm and resolute during the negotiations and planning, I only had to call up the image of that old aunt in the corner, peeling piles of potatoes.

Chapter 3 — May 20

My Pod was gone, and Barb's had arrived. The neighbors watched the pickup and delivery with the same interest as the first time the technical wonder had appeared at our place.

One couple, in particular, couldn't stop talking about it. Jack and Ted lived just down the street from us. They had been the first to welcome us to our new home when they appeared within an hour of our arrival with a loaf of home-baked bread and a stick of butter.

They had been partners for over twenty years before they moved to Vermont to get married. Jack was tall and slight, with short gray hair and glasses normally worn at the end of his nose so he could see over the top of them. He hated bifocals, he said. They were for old people. Ted was a blonde, with piercing blue eyes that opened widely in mock innocence before he delivered, deadpan, a zinger. Both were in their early sixties.

"Ruth, do you think we could rent a Pod to just sit in the front yard, even if we don't move it anywhere?" Jack asked as he watched Barb's Pod be delivered.

I nodded, "Sure. People do it all the time if they're remodeling or doing some sort of construction. They can move their stuff into the Pod to get it out of the way for a while, and keep it safe and clean. Why? Are you planning to remodel?"

Ted shook his head, a glint in his eye. "No. I just want to see that young man climb around on the truck a couple more times."

Jack rolled his eyes. "God, Ted. Shut up! Yes, Ruth, we're going to re-carpet the entire downstairs. I am just sick to death of having to look at that dark mocha morass every day. I want something lighter. More taupe with a touch of khaki."

Ted looked to the heavens, slightly shaking his head. He heaved a sigh, then said, "Let's wait until the first of July. It will be hotter then. Maybe the delivery guy will have to take off his shirt."

Jack moved closer to me, turning his back on Ted. "He gets worse all the time. I can hardly take him out in public anymore."

I laughed. "You guys want some coffee? You can look at Barb's color swatches."

Jack nodded amiably, but Ted declined. He said he needed to go write more letters to the legislature. As he turned toward his home, he fluttered fingers over his shoulder. "Later," he called, cheerfully.

"He's a real activist," Jack informed me. "He spends hours every day working on causes he thinks are important. He was so excited about the Supreme Court striking down the Defense of Marriage Act, DOMA, you know, that he cried for three days."

We opened the heavy Dutch-door into Barb's living room where every surface was covered with fabric samples and paint swatches. Jack looked around, clapped his hands in glee, and said, "Heaven!"

Barb wandered in from the kitchen. "Oh, Jack, I'm glad you're here. Ruthie gets tired of looking at colors much faster than I do. And I know what she wants, anyway – a color with a good, propitious name. She likes that pale gold because it's called 'A Sensible Hue', and the off-white because it's 'Vermont Cream.' I ask you, can you imagine picking colors by their names?"

Jack looked at me in mock dismay. "Go away, dearie, and let us grownups work. Fetch us some coffee." He turned back to Barb and said happily, "Well. I think the first thing you need to do is decide if you're going cool or warm. Then you can sort your samples into piles appropriate to each tonal group."

I shook my head in amusement as I walked into the dining room and opened the door to the connecting hall between our houses. It was a convenient passageway, although it had initially been the source of a little disagreement between Barb and me.

Let me back up and describe this "dual living house" that we bought.

The two houses are similar: each is a story and a half, post and beam construction, about 2000 square feet. Each has kitchen, living, dining, bath on the first floor and two bedrooms and a bath upstairs. The configuration of the rooms is different in each but the overall feel is the same – Federal-style with a large central fireplace.

My house is on the left (south) and sits with its gables perpendicular to the street and a full-length covered porch providing a vantage of the neighborhood with its joggers and dog-walkers. Barb's sits gable-end to the street and has only a stoop leading to the very ornate front entrance. My side was the home of the carpenter or joiner who built both houses; Barb's was his carpentry shop.

Between the two houses is a seven-foot square connecting room. It had been closed off when we bought the house. I wanted to open it up to allow us to go back and forth without having to go outside. Barb was opposed. She thought we should leave the structure alone, as it had been built.

I finally convinced her that our carpenter, Josiah Lake, would not have built a closed connector between his home and shop. It must have been closed when the two houses were sold separately in the 1850s. She finally agreed. We opened it.

My side of the connector opened into the hallway off my kitchen. Just beside the door to the breakfast room, I had created a charging station for my iPhone, iPad, and cordless home phone. The voicemail lights were blinking on both phones as I walked past them on my way to get the coffee.

"Good," I thought, "maybe somebody finally called me back." I had spent the morning calling contractors, carpenters, chimney sweeps, masons, electricians, plumbers, and painters. I had reached none.

Barb and I had decided on a division of labor. She was better with decorating trivia and I was better at managing contacts, estimates, and contracts. And I would use voice mail.

So I dialed my voice mail on the speaker phone while I poured three cups of coffee. Callbacks from the sweep and the mason had come in. Both houses have beautiful fireplaces we were afraid to light and deteriorating stone steps. We needed help.

I left a "Now it's your turn" message for the mason but actually caught the sweep and set up an appointment. Small victories keep me going.

As I carried the coffee back to Barb's, I could hear Jack waxing eloquent about the virtues of pure white trim. "You can repaint only the rooms that need it, but use the pure white. Then eventually they'll all be done. And it won't limit you to any wall color. You can go warm or cool; light or dark. And still get adequate contrast."

"OK, guys. Can you hold off further color theory explorations for a few minutes and drink your coffee before it gets cold? And, Barb, before I forget, the sweep's coming Tuesday."

"Oh, good. This is such a beautiful fireplace. I can't wait to light a blazing fire in it. It will be so lovely sitting here in my newly upholstered warm-sand-colored leather recliner watching the fire while the snow flies outside the window."

I nodded and cocked an eyebrow. Lord, she could go on.

Jack finished his coffee, kissed Barb on the cheek, nodded to me and left.

Barb smiled, "He's the dearest man. Do you know what he told me? Remember the day we first looked at the houses and Ted came by with their old dog? He was checking us out. To see if we were a couple or at least gay-friendly. Isn't that adorable?"

"I'm not sure 'adorable' is the word I'd choose. But it is sort of funny. So what did he decide?"

"He figured we weren't a couple. He thought I was a good possibility, but you weren't."

"Now that is funny," I said.

Barb wrinkled her brow as she glanced at me, but didn't reply.

Chapter 4 — June 1

"Barb, come here. We got the written report from the chimney sweep," I yelled as I slit open the envelope.

"Well, he took his sweet time getting it to us. What's he say?"

"Oh-oh," I muttered as I scanned the letter from Chip the Sweep. "He says our chimneys are in bad shape. We can't light fires in them." I read on, letting out a groan as I handed the letter to Barb. "Here, see for yourself."

"Oh, no! 'Furnace of north house uses same flue as the fireplace.' 'Inadvisable to live in house with the furnace on.' 'Leaking carbon monoxide into the second floor.' 'Possibly deadly.' So what do we do?" She sat down hard at the kitchen table, her left hand over her mouth.

"That's on the last page: tear down the chimney and rebuild it. Estimated cost – $30,000."

"What? You must have misread it. Let me see." She flipped through the pages of the report. "Nope. You're not wrong. So what DO we do?"

"I think I start calling people. Surely our only options are not for you to asphyxiate or freeze to death." I strode off purposefully to retrieve my iPad, but I was as shaken as Barb. What had we done? Had we bought a bottomless money pit? I needed to find that inspection report we'd had done. It didn't mention death-trap anywhere, I was sure.

I called several people, including the contractor who was going to give us a bid on rebuilding my front porch. He said he planned to look at the porch in the next few days and he'd look at the chimney, too. Maybe there was a third option cheaper than $30,000.

It wasn't much, but I did tell Barb the news. She looked at me sadly and said, "Is it feed a cold, starve a fever, and drown your sorrows?"

"I think so. How about a cold beer or a glass of wine?"

Barb nodded. "Yes. Let's go to the pub." The pub was faux-Irish with uncharming decor and mediocre food, but it had the attraction of being only two blocks away.

A couple of pints and a sandwich left us calmer if only temporarily anesthetized. As we neared the sidewalk to our houses, I heard the phone ring and sprinted to answer it. "Hello!" I gasped as I grabbed it.

"Something wrong with you?" Belle Sheppard asked sharply. "Seriously, Ruth, you OK?"

"I'm fine. Just had to dash for the phone. Goodness, it's wonderful to hear your voice. Is everything all right with you? And Sally?" Belle and Sally were friends from Oklahoma.

"Yes, we're fine. Just too damned hot in this God-forsaken state. Forget everything I said about your moving. In fact, we were wondering if you were up for guests any time soon. We're thinking of coming your way in early July, if that works for you."

"Hell, yes, that works for me! I miss you two cantankerous old women! As long as you don't mind being in the middle of a construction zone, we'd love to have you. Any time in July is fine with me. Let me check with Barb." I had walked back into the living room where Barb had settled as I spoke. As I raised my eyebrows at her, she nodded."Barb says so, too. We will probably have workers here every day working on the porch, though."

"Good Lord, Ruth, you know we don't mind piddly stuff like that." That was Sally. "I'm on, too. Can't trust Belle to give me all the details. Have to listen for myself."

I grinned."Of course you do, Sally. As I said before, come any time. One thing, though, Sally. How's your knee doing? All the bedrooms are upstairs. But I could make up a daybed in the living room, if your knee won't take steep New England stairs."

"Now, don't fuss. I can handle the stairs as long as I don't have to run up and down them. That massage therapist I found in Enid is doing me a world of good," Sally assured me.

"She's telling the truth, Ruth," Belle affirmed. "She's walking better now than she has in years."

"Then it's settled. You are coming. Just pick the dates and let me know." I was smiling so much my cheeks were starting to ache. I love Sally and Belle.

"Then let's just be tidy and arrive on July 1. How's that?" Belle asked.

"Perfect," I replied. "And stay a while."

"Hell's bells, honey! You'll be sick of us in 3 days," Sally cackled.

"You know better than that! And I can't wait for you two to meet Barb. I think you will really like her."

Belle interrupted Sally who started to agree with me, "OK, then. We will arrive at your house on July 1. We may drive up, see a bit of the country. But if we fly, we'll rent a car. You won't have to fetch us from anywhere."

I could tell Belle was getting antsy to end the call. Two to three minutes were generally her limit. But she surprised me by asking a final question: "Um, Ruth. I forgot to ask. Do you have a fenced yard?"

"Uh, yes. A big one," I replied. "Why?"

"Just curious," Belle said quickly. "Now we'll talk to you later when we've firmed everything up." And she hung up quickly, without giving me a chance to sign off. That was Belle.

I put the phone down and turned to Barb. "Sally and Belle are coming to visit, as I guess you heard."

"That's great, Ruthie, but they can't stay here. My chimney isn't safe."

"I know this is Vermont, Barb, but I seriously doubt we will need a fire in early July." I grinned at her.

"Oh! Right! We'll have time to find a solution before we need heat. I hope." She took a breath. "OK. So refresh my memory. Are Sally and Belle the ones who own the diner or the kennel?"

"The kennel. It's an absolutely wonderful place that specializes in breeding and training border collies and bloodhounds. Belle handles the border collies and Sally does the bloodhounds. They've been in business together for years. They call their place BellWhether Kennels."

"Odd name," Barb said.

"Yep. It's a long story. Belle Sheppard was not her original name. Her last name was Bell. She wanted to change it to keep a crazy ex-husband from finding her. Sally always called her by her last name, Bell, and said she'd call her Bell whether or not it was her legal name. BellWhether. Get it?"

Barb replied dryly, "Yes, Ruth. I get it. What's Sally's last name?"

"O'Neill. She's older, livelier, messier and more effusive. Belle is taller, thinner, tidier, and more reserved. And they're both great. I think you'll like them."

"I'm sure I will. Oh, this will be fun. Our first house guests. And if you want, you can put one of them in my spare room so they don't have to share," Barb offered.

"Thanks. That's nice. My first inclination is to put them together at my place, but they might like some privacy. Let me think about it."

"That gives us an incentive to get the interior painting done. At least the places where the hideous wallpaper needs to be covered up. Have you decided if you want white or off-white trim? And what color for the dining room? That orange-flowered mess has got to go. You know, Jack had a great idea. He thought you should paint it silver-gray to complement the china in the corner cabinet. But of course, if you do that, you really need to use pure white trim."

"Oh, Barb. Stop. You are making my head hurt." I dramatically rubbed my temples to let her know I was serious. She could get so wound up over decorating! I really don't get it.

"OK. OK. Just promise you will actually look at the paint swatches and not just pick the color based on its name."

"It works with race horses," I muttered.

Chapter 5 — July 4

"What do you wear to a town picnic?" Sally called down the stairs. Sally, of the if-it's-clean-and covers-me-up-it's-fine fashion philosophy was asking me what to wear. Hmm.

"Damned if I know," I shouted back. "I've never been to one before."

"Then I guess it's going to be jeans and a cotton shirt. OK?"

"Sure, sounds great. Come out back when you're ready. Belle's going to give me and Sojo a lesson. I have to get the jumps."

Sally and Belle had arrived, as planned, on July 1. But they were not alone. They had with them a beautiful, four-year-old border collie named BellWhether's Sojourner. Sojo's previous owner, Sandy, had tearfully given Sojo to Belle as she left for a three-year assignment in China. Sandy and Sojo had been traveling companions while Sandy drove around a four-state area supporting her networking clients and attending agility trials. But a new job with a new home-base in Beijing precluded Sojo. Belle had promised to find a perfect home for her. She thought mine was it.

Belle told me more than once that I didn't have to accept Sojo, but that if I did, I had to promise to work with her in agility. I knew what dog agility was — I had seen Belle work her dogs at climbing A-frames, jumping thru tires, running through tunnels — but I had never tried it. Belle told me that Sojo was well-trained, but I wasn't. I had to learn how to steer the dog at full speed using only my gestures and voice.

Belle had a two-part plan to get me trained. She would work with me on the basics while she was here, and she had arranged with a trainer friend to take me on after she and Sally left. So we had built a few simple obstacles from PVC pipe, three jumps and weave poles. She said Sojo knew how to do all the obstacles, and I could learn the basics with just a few.

I dragged the jumps to the middle of the yard and positioned them in a straight line about 10 feet apart, as Belle directed. She told me to get Sojo and put her in a stay about five feet behind the first jump. "Palm facing her nose with your fingers up means Stay," Belle reminded me. "Now run out about halfway between the first and second jumps, on the right side of them." I complied.

"Next, you have to do a couple things simultaneously, so listen before you move. You want to plant your feet perpendicular to the line you want Sojo to run between the two jumps. Then turn your body toward her while straightening out your left arm. Then tell her 'OK' and 'Jump' as you swing your arm from pointing at her to pointing beyond the jump you want her to take. Got it? Try it."

I did. It worked. Sojo shot forward, jumped the first jump and stopped in front of me, waiting for further instructions.

"Wow! Wow!" I said. "Now what?"

"Give her a treat. She'll run for approval, but she'll run happier for food."

I gave her small pieces of cheese as Belle gave me my next instructions. She said, "Put her back in the start position and tell her to stay. You're going to do exactly the same thing you did before except, when you see that she's committed to jumping the first jump, start running past the second jump, sweep your left arm forward, and say 'Jump' again, then stop about half way between the second and third jumps. And treat her."

I did. It worked again.

"Now, same thing, but go past the third jump with another 'Jump' command." Belle smiled. "Fun, huh?"

"Big fun." I did as Belle had directed and successfully got Sojo through three jumps. I was delighted. "Now I see why people do this. It's great," I enthused.

"I thought you'd like it. It gets harder when you steer through more difficult twists and turns, but the fun and satisfaction are usually proportional with the complexity." Belle said seriously.

I laughed. "That sounds very profound."

Belle nodded. "It is. Almost everything you need to know about life you can learn from training dogs." She looked directly at Sojo who was sitting at my side, watching to see what I wanted her to do next. "Sojo, that'll do."

Sojo lay down and looked intently at Belle. "I just told her that we're done with this activity and getting ready to do something else."

"Doggie shorthand?" I quipped.

"Sure. That's what commands are. Shorthand ways to tell your dog what you want her to do. Just remember, Sojo knows a lot more than you. You'll have to work hard to keep up." She looked again at Sojo. "OK, girl. Good girl. Come." A love fest ensued.

Belle patted Sojo a last time before turning toward the house. "I need to get ready for the picnic. I'll set up a time when we can go to the agility field and let you try a few more obstacles. OK?"

I nodded as I hugged Sojo. "God, you're a cool dog! You are absolutely the coolest dog I have ever known." I headed back to the house, Sojo at my side, nuzzling my hand as I walked.

Sally walked down to meet us. "Are you in love yet?"

"Almost. Totally infatuated." I replied.

"Good. Take your time. Make the right decision for yourself. Now, let's go to a picnic."

After we got home from the picnic, we all congregated on Barb's back deck. Barb started telling stories of plumbers and masons and sweeps. Oh, my!

"So Stan, our contractor, said he thought there was a third option to my freezing to death or asphyxiating. A direct vent. It sucks the exhaust from the furnace through a pipe that goes directly outdoors. Totally bypasses the death-trap chimney. He was right. We got it fixed for about a thousand dollars. Sounds like a lot until you compare it to the thirty thousand to rebuild the chimney," Barb said.

"That's great, Barb. Sounds like you found a good contractor. And looks like it, too. They're doing a beautiful job on Ruth's porch." Sally poured another glass of iced tea. "You going to use him for other stuff?"

"Probably," I replied, "he's going to give us a bid for painting the house and fixing the rot. I'm getting three bids, so we'll see how he comes in."

"You two have been swamped with house stuff. What are you going to do when that's all finished?" Belle asked seriously.

Barb replied thoughtfully, "I've been thinking about that. I've kind of gotten interested in who built this house and what it was like here during the 1820s and 30s. I thought I might check out the historical society. They might have something…." Her voice drifted off into uncertainty as she caught my eye.

"Really? I didn't know that," I said.

"I just started thinking about it the last few days."

"What about you, Ruth?" Sally asked.

I mock-sighed. "I guess I'll be learning agility from Sojo."

"Poor thing," Sally crooned.

I grinned. "I don't know. It seems like I have a 'Tell-me-your-life-story' face. I have heard some of the most amazing tales from folks I've met here. I've been thinking about writing some of them down." I shrugged.

"I know!" Sally blurted. "Can you rhyme? Write The Centerbury Tales!"

I declaimed in a slow, deep voice:

"We bought an ancient house in Centerb'ry;
And then began to make required repairs;
But ev'ry thing we did was far from free;
So now we're at the edge of deep despair."

Everyone chuckled, advising me to give up rhyme. But Belle looked as me appraisingly and said, "You know, I'd hate to see you give up on writing. You were doing so well last fall."

"Thanks, Belle. Maybe I will. But first, my other task. What time do we go to the agility field tomorrow? Sojo and I need to get prepared."

"Noon. But how do you get prepared?"

I called Sojo to my side. "I don't know. I thought maybe she'd tell me. Won't you girl?" I kissed her cheek and pounded her side. She nuzzled my neck and wagged her tail.

Sally looked on approvingly. "I think the infatuation is mutual."

Chapter 6 — July 29

Barb's dive into discovering the history of our house was more like a wade. She was fairly unambitious. She made a couple of trips to the town and county historical societies but she mainly played with paint colors and fabric swatches. I'm not sure what she planned to recover, but she and Jack seemed to find plenty to discuss.

I had decided to paint my entire place white with antique white trim. I wanted the light from the windows reflected everywhere, and the creamy antique white next to bright white was a pleasing but subtle contrast. Or so I thought.

After spending thirty minutes on that decision, I left all discussion of color, tone, texture, and value to Barb and Jack. Ted joined in on occasion.

I spent much of my time with Sojo. We went to class each week and practiced in the backyard several times in between classes. In addition, I had ordered several training DVDs that I watched assiduously, practicing turning my hips, shoulders, and feet in the direction that Sojo could read correctly.

I even hung a big mirror in my living room so I could watch my movements. Jack and Ted made endless fun of me as they postured in contortions while calling me to Come or Jump. I laughed good-naturedly but grew more determined to enter a trial with Sojo in the fall to prove to myself and them that I could do it.

One problem I had was that Sojo was an experienced dog with titles behind her name. And I was not an experienced handler. I needed to be at the beginner level, but she was well beyond beginner skills and could not complete at a level below her titles.

When I mentioned my problem to Brenda, my trainer, she chuckled, "Not a problem. You just need to start in another venue." I must have looked puzzled because she explained further, "There are several groups who sponsor agility trials. AKC, USDAA, NADAC, CPE, etc. Sojo has titles in AKC. You just need to start her as a beginner in one of the other groups."

I really didn't understand the alphabet soup, but I did get that I didn't have the problem I thought I had. I began to practice even more seriously.

But it wasn't easy. After the training session I'd had earlier that day when I had gotten lost on the course, tripped over the wing of a jump and nearly went through one of the tunnels feet first, I was feeling particularly glum. I began making a list to give to Belle of all the reasons I should keep Sojo but stop agility training. I was having trouble convincing even myself.

Luckily, Barb interrupted me. "Ruth, you won't believe what I found." Barb said breathlessly as she hurried into my living room holding something very dirty in her hand.

"Let me see," I said, reaching out toward a rusty-looking metal box.

"Not so fast. Let me catch my breath." She sat down next to me on the sofa. "You know that Jess and Bill have been taking down my evil chimney and roofing over the hole, right?"

I nodded. It was hard to miss the noise of bricks thrown into the back of a pickup truck or hammering that rattles the china.

"So I got to wondering if their tearing down the outside of the chimney might dislodge anything. I went into the cellar and looked around the fireplace there, in the summer kitchen. Oh, isn't it lovely to have a summer kitchen? And that fireplace is so charming. It's such a shame we can't use it. Nor the one above it." She sighed.

"Barb," I asked patiently, "what did you find?"

"Oh," she looked down at her hands, "this rusty box, along with about a bushel of acorns, fell out when I pulled off the board that blocked the flue. I can't get it open. Do you have any WD-40?"

I went to the laundry room and rummaged through my tool basket until I found a small can of penetrating oil. "No WD-40, but this ought to work," I said as I returned. I dripped oil around the band of the lid. "Let it sit a minute," I ordered.

"Oh, isn't this exciting? What do you think might be in it? I can hardly wait to see," Barb bubbled. "Do you think it's ready yet?"

"Probably not, but I'll try," I conceded. I wiggled and pulled on the lid and finally got it to budge a little. Its shape made it difficult to maneuver. It was rather like tugging on a brick about three inches deep and four inches tall and wide. The top slid down over part of the bottom which was slightly smaller and had a raised band that stopped the top from going on too far.

"Oh, give it here," Barb demanded. "I can't stand it." She wiggled, pulled, rocked, and cursed the lid before she finally pulled it off and peered inside.

"What's in it?" I asked.

"I'm not sure," Barb mumbled as she extracted a yellowed, tightly rolled piece of paper and a stained cloth bag. She carefully unrolled the paper, studied it with a frown, then opened the bag and gasped.

"What? Dammit, what?" I demanded.

Barb's eyebrows were pulled together in puzzlement as she said, "The paper says, 'More where this came from.' and the bag has, well, it looks like a gold nugget." She stretched out her hand, palm up, to display what certainly did look like a gold nugget.

I sat down next to her and examined both the paper and the nugget. "Now, tell me again where you found this?"

"I opened up the flue in the little fireplace in the cellar you know, the summer kitchen. This fell out."

"Have you ever opened up the flue before?"

"No."

"So you have no way of knowing if it was lying there for years or was just dislodged by the deconstruction."

"That's right." Barb placed the paper and nugget back inside the box. "Do you have a zipper bag I can put these in?"

I fetched a bag from the kitchen and held it open for Barb to slide the box inside. She sealed it and laid it on the table beside her.

"Damn!" Barb marveled. "Damn! Do you think that's really gold? How can I find out?"

"I don't know. In the old Westerns, there was always an assayer's office. I don't know what the modern equivalent is. County Extension?"

Barb picked up my iPad from the table beside me and Googled "gold assay." She found entries for fire assaying, chemical assaying, and electronic assaying. Assaying kits, kilns and caboodles. She finally found her way to the Vermont Geological Society and their list of testing labs. She grabbed the phone and called the first on the list.

"Hello, my name is Barbara King. I live in Centerbury and have found what appears to be a gold nugget in my old house here. Can you tell me what I need to do to get it tested to see if it's really gold?" She fiddled with the plastic bag as she spoke.

"No, it's a small nugget. About a half-inch in diameter, I guess." She paused and listened then mimed pencil and paper to me. I handed her my notebook. She wrote as she repeated, "Plymouth Assayers, 802-555-1212. Yes, I have it. Thanks." She lay down the phone and leaned back against the sofa.

"OK," she said, speaking quickly, "they said that many jewelers have electronic assay equipment. Or I could take it to a testing lab where they could do a thorough analysis, telling me the complete makeup of the sample. The closest one is in Plymouth. Do you know where that is?"

I picked up the iPad and in a few seconds replied, "Near Rutland. The birthplace of Calvin Coolidge. About an hour from here."

"Hmm. I guess I'll try the jeweler first. Do you want to come along?"

"Sure."

"OK. Let's go."

Within a few minutes we were in the town's only jewelry store asking the jeweler if she could and would test Barb's nugget.

"Yes, I can test it, said Jodie Goldstone, the thirty-something Birkenstock-wearing jeweler. "I won't charge you this time, but if you start bringing me more yellow pebbles to test, I will. People seem to think it's funny to get someone named Goldstone to test their pebbles."

"Oh, OK. Thanks." Barb handed over the questionable yellow pebble.

"It's going to take a few minutes. Why don't you wander over to Delia's and get a coffee or something?" She said over her shoulder as she walked into her workroom.

Delia's is the local coffee house/deli. I ordered coffees for each of us while Barb snagged a table. We sipped coffee and said little for about ten minutes until Barb jumped up and said, "That's it. I can't wait longer. I'm going back."

Jodie Goldstone was waiting for us. "I am amazed," she said, "but this little rock comes in at 23.5 carats. That's about 96% pure. Purest nugget I've ever seen. Where did you say you got it?"

"I found it in my house when that rusty can fell out of my chimney."

"Nice find. With today's price of gold, this little pebble is worth several hundred dollars. May I see the can it was in? I've got a mild acid bath that might help us figure out what used to be printed on that old tobacco tin."

I handed her the tin, saying, "Tobacco tin? Is that what it is?"

"I think so," Jodie replied. "Let me see. She carried it into the back room and was back within a few minutes with a much cleaner box, painted a pale yellow with drawings of two men and lettering that said "1860 Old Virginia Sm". The bottom right corner was illegible with rust, but it looked like it might say "Smoke."

Jodie looked excited. She went to her laptop and typed a few words before swinging the screen toward us. It contained and image of a tin like ours, only much cleaner.

"The time fits," she said. "There was a mini-gold rush here in Vermont starting in the late 1850s. Up in Plymouth."

Barb looked thunderstruck. I thanked Ms. Goldstone, bagged the nugget, and steered Barb out of the shop.

As we walked back to our house, Barb seemed to wake from here daze. "I am going to figure this out," she announced firmly. "Josiah Lake wants me to."

Chapter 7 — August 18

The first couple weeks of August were Barb's personal Gold Rush. After she found out her nugget was real, she turned into a history-hunting hurricane. She hounded the historical societies, she convinced Chip the Sweep to bring back his flashlight camera and shine it up the chimney to see if any more treasure lay hidden inside. She went to the cellar and minutely examined every nook, shelf, cranny, and mouse hole. She found mouse turds, shredded paper, string, and sunflower seed shells.

I stayed out of her way. I was dealing with furnace replacement, slow-draining bathtubs, and a cobbled-together wiring system that frequently left me in the dark when I turned on even the most innocuous appliance like a radio. I knew there were some problems with the electric service; they had been identified in our inspection report. But there are problems and then there are problems!

I had just recovered from learning that the electric dryer and electric range were on the same circuit that was drastically undersized to handle either, when Barb came in carrying a stack of papers and a tall glass of ice.

"Have you got anything I can put in this?" she asked, holding out her glass.

I laughed. "There's another hard cider in the fridge. It's what I'm having. Another great thing about living in Vermont. They make this stuff here." Barb dropped her stack of papers on the table next to me and went after her drink.

I glanced at the top page. It was titled, Josiah Lake, and contained a brief biographical detail of the man who had built the house in which I was sitting:

- Born 1798, Troy, NY   Died 1895, Centerbury, VT
- Worked with brother, Oliver, carpenter & joiner   1815-23
- Bought land in Centerbury 1821
- Began work on shop 1821. Completed 1823
- Began work on house 1823. Completed 1827.
- Married Sophia Harrison 1827
- Sophia died 1852. No living children.
- Josiah disappeared 1857 - 61

I had of course seen the historic information plaque on the corner of my house every time I went in or out the front door, but I had spent little time thinking about who Josiah Lake was. Barb's list of facts about him finally caught my attention.

"So, what else do you know about Josiah besides these few facts?" I asked as Barb settled into the chair beside me. "Where did he disappear to?"

"I'm forming a theory about that. I need to get a book from inter-library loan first. But I'll tell you what I know." She paused for a long swallow of cider.

"OK. I've found a few stories about Josiah in a couple of contemporary diaries. As a young man he was a 'gay blade.' Liked to dress up in the most outrageously fashionable style. Big legged pants, bright colors. He was a flirt and a prankster. He once painted his neighbor's white cow blue. Caused quite a stir.

"He settled down when he fell in love with Sophia Harrison. Her parents didn't like him. Thought he was too unsteady to marry their only daughter. So he set about proving them wrong, buying land, building a carpentry shop and a house, and becoming a respected member of the community. They finally married in 1827 when he finished the house. I guess it was enough to convince her parents.

"I didn't find much about him during the next thirty years except that he bought and sold property and was involved in lending and borrowing money in connection with his carpentry business. It looks like he built a lot of houses and other buildings.

"Then Sophia died in 1857, leaving no living children. No telling how many babies she actually had. Childhood mortality was so high then. I think only about a third made it to adulthood. Or she might have had stillbirths. Or they died at some point before she did. Or I suppose she or Josiah could have been sterile. Women's lives are much less accessible in public records than men's. Men tended to do things that get recorded – buy things, sell things, build things. But about the only public things women did was be born, get married, and die. They had children, but it's hard to find children's names listed with their mothers. Only their fathers. You'd think they had sprung full-formed from their father's heads, like Athena, for all the credit the mothers get."

Barb finally paused long enough for me to interrupt. "OK, I understand the lack of domestic history. But what's your theory about Josiah's disappearance?"

"Well, I still have to do some checking to see if it's feasible given the travel times and train routes, or ships. Ships! I hadn't thought about ships before. He could have taken a ship." She grabbed her stack of papers, shuffled through the top layer until she found what she was looking for. She made a few notes on the page she'd found before putting it back into the stack. "Wow. I had no idea. Did you know that you could get from New York to San Francisco in just 23 days in 1855?"

"No, Barb, I didn't know that. And what does that have to do with the price of rice in China?"

Barb looked totally nonplussed. "Why, nothing. Whatever are you talking about, Ruth?"

"Oh, never mind. What's your theory?" I asked patiently.

"Oh, I think he went to Boston or New York and worked there a while. Then, maybe, took a steamer to Panama, crossed the Isthmus on the Panama Railway, and took another steamer to California. In 23 days.

"Gold was discovered in 1848 and even as late as 1855 hordes of fortune hunters still flocked to the gold fields. But I wonder if Josiah might have gone as a builder rather than a miner. San Fran had grown from about 500 people before 1848 to about 50,000 by 1855. All those people needed buildings. He could have made his fortune in his own trade."

"Wow, that's quite a theory. How can you prove it?" I asked.

"I think I can find passenger lists for steamers arriving in San Francisco. I just need to narrow down the time frame. Somehow."

"Could you find out how much passage would cost and work backwards? Figure out how long it would take him to earn passage money? Or do you think he had the money when he left here?"

"I don't know. Maybe he mortgaged his house or something. I wasn't really looking for that when I was digging through the town records." She made a few notes then stood up abruptly. "See you later. I have a lot of work to do."

Now she'd piqued my interest. I picked up my iPad and did a little research. I found that only about twenty-five ships from Panama arrived in San Francisco during 1858. Looking through passenger lists for twenty-five ships couldn't be that hard. And maybe she could get Ted and Jack to help. They could discuss interior paint colors while they searched.

I leaned back in my recliner, took another sip of cider, and grinned. It was good to see Barb excited about something even though she did tend to lecture.

I was tired. I'd been out early with Sojo for our lesson. I settled back into the chair and closed my eyes. I was just starting to slide into sleep when my phone rang.

"Hello," I mumbled.

"Is this Ruth Welborne?"

"Yes."

"This is Mary Nell Floyd. I'm Belle Sheppard's daughter. And I need some help."

Chapter 8 — August 29

Mary Nell Floyd looked so much like her mother I had to stop myself from calling her "Belle". "Looks like you made it," I said with a smile. "1700 miles! You should be totally frazzled, but you look like you just took a cool shower."

"Oh, it's easy to look cool when the temps are in the 70s. We left 102 two days ago." She gave me a quick hug and whispered in my ear, "I can never thank you enough. I'll tell you about it later." She pulled back and said loudly, "Walter! Bitsy! We're over here!"

But the next person I saw wasn't Mary Nell's husband, Walter, nor her granddaughter, Bitsy. It was my great-nephew, Jake. He looked like he'd grown at least an inch since I saw him in May. His black curls bounced as he blasted up the sidewalk and launched himself at me. I caught him, without falling, while trying to respond to his barrage of questions.

"Did you miss me, Aunt Ruthie? Are you surprised to see me? I didn't tell nobody I was coming. And guess what, Aunt Ruthie. I'm FIVE now!"

"Jakey Boy!" I nuzzled his neck. "I am so surprised! I knew Mary Nell, Walter, and Bitsy were coming, but I had no idea you were, too! Wow! I am so happy to see you, but I have to put you down. You have gotten heavy! And so big! Five years old!"

I set Jake down, holding onto his ever-sticky hand, and turned to greet my other visitors.

Jake dropped my hand and ran down the walk toward a blonde sprite dancing around beside a tall, slightly portly man with a wide smile and odd-colored eyes – one blue and one brown. "Bitsy! Gramps! Come meet my Aunt Ruthie!" Jake sang my name as he jumped across the walk and dashed back to the porch.

"Gramps?" I asked Mary Nell.

"Bitsy calls us Gramps and Grandmary. Jake picked it up. We like it. You don't mind?" Mary Nell glanced quickly at me.

"I think it's terrific." I stepped forward, extending my hand, "I'm Ruth Welborne," I told the advancing Walter.

"I feel like I know you," he said with a mischievous grin. "I've heard your praises sung for 1700 miles."

"We didn't sing praises, silly Gramps," the skipping blonde sprite said. "We sang SONGS!"

"You must be Bitsy," I told her as I leaned toward her.

She looked at me closely, squinted, closed her brown eye and peered at me through her blue one. "Yep," she nodded, "and you're Aunt Ruthie," she declaimed solemnly. She stepped closer and hugged me around the waist. She was a disconcerting child.

"Aunt Ruthie," Jake interrupted my thoughts, "Momma said you have a doggie."

"Yes, I do. Her name is Sojo. Bitsy's Grandma Belle brought her to me. She's in the back yard. You two want to go play with her?" I started toward the back yard, children in tow. "I'll be right back," I told Mary Nell and Walter, "or you two can come along and take a look at our place."

They followed. I described the features of the house as we walked. The kids ran circles around us singing "Hurry Up, Hurry Up, Hurry Up!"

Walter looked at the house carefully, touched some of the woodwork, and looked pleased.

When we got to the backyard, Sojo was bouncing at the gate. I picked up a ball and tossed it to Jake. "Why don't you two go play ball with Sojo. She needs the exercise."

"Oh, boy!" Jake shouted as he threw a long ball to the center of the yard. Sojo and Bitsy ran to retrieve it. Sojo got there first, but she dropped the ball at Bitsy's feet and crouched in front of her, waiting.

"You could tell from her shadow that she's a border collie," Walter observed, pointing at the classic crouched shape in the late afternoon shadows.

I nodded. "I've never had a border collie before. This one is pretty special."

Walter looked at me seriously. "You've got a problem now. No other dog will ever measure up. Border collies spoil you for any other dog."

Mary Nell laughed. "You love saying that, don't you?" She turned to me, "An old farmer told Walter that years ago, and he repeats it to everyone."

"Well, it's true," Walter retorted. "You should see Bitsy's dog, Heart. That is one smart dog. Bitsy's nuts about her, and she is Bitsy's self-appointed guard, playmate, and soul mate."

Mary Nell winked at Walter, "And Bitsy's the only one who likes her, huh?" She looked to me and continued, "Heart lives with us, so she has the run of the farm. Bitsy comes over nearly every day to play with her. We all love that puppy Belle picked out for Bits."

"Jake has a dog, Oliver. He's a magical corgi," I chuckled, remembering Jake's dream of getting a puppy just when Oliver showed up.

"Belle told me that story. Pretty amazing. Has he dreamed up anything else?"

I nodded, "I think he did. A dad. Isn't Win perfect?" I asked.

"I just met him once, but I liked him. Why does Jake call him 'Daddy Bear'?" Walter asked.

"His real name is Winston, but nearly everyone calls him 'Win' except for the kids he went to high school with. They call him 'Smoke.' Jake turned it into 'Smoky,' then 'Smoky Bear.' When Win and my niece, Janie, got married, Win told Jake he'd like to be a real dad to him. Right after that, Jake started calling Win 'Daddy Bear.' It tickles Win."

Walter walked closer to the house and ran his fingers down the corner pilaster. "This is beautiful. It was built in the 1820s?"

"Yes. Josiah Lake built both these houses. He lived in this one and used the other for his carpentry shop. If you want to know all the details, wait until you meet Barb. She'll inundate you with the history of this place."

"I'll inundate whom with what?" Barb said as she rounded the corner. "Hi, I'm Barbara King," she said to Mary Nell and Walter. "You must be Belle's daughter. You look like her." She took Mary Nell's hand then pulled her into a hug. "I love your mother," she said quietly. "And you're the husband, Walter," she said, turning to him. "I am so happy to meet you both."

I don't know why I hadn't noticed it before, but Barb looked enough like Mary Nell to be her sister. Same short gray hair, same buxom figure, same straight posture and I'll-brook-no-nonsense demeanor. I don't think Barb knows much about her extended family. Wouldn't it be something if…. I shook myself back to the present.

Barb was saying, "You must be pooped. I thought you could stay at my place and let the kids stay with Ruth. Does that suit?"

"No, no!" Walter said quickly. "We will go to a hotel. Or Mary Nell, Bitsy and I will. Jake can stay here with Aunt Ruthie."

"Nonsense," Barb announced in a voice that had handled 30 years of classroom nonsense. "We have plenty of room. Come and I'll show you the way."

Walter shrugged and followed meekly. Mary Nell grinned, "He's used to being bossed around."

Jake came in just then and said, "Aunt Barb fits right in."

Barb grinned as she turned away. She had been nobody's Aunt Barb until now.

After dinner, I got Jake into the shower. Mary Nell insisted that Bitsy, too, needed to bathe. "But Grandmary," Bitsy said, "can't I take a BATH instead of a SHOWER. I saw a bathtub as big as a swimming pool. And I could be the princess. And you could bring me grapes while I soak in bubbles."

Mary Nell shook her head in amusement, "We'll have to check with Ruth."

"Oh, please, Aunt Ruthie, can I take a Princess Bath?" Bitsy asked, doing her best to look like a Princess.

"Of course you may. Let me see if I have any bubble bath."

Mary Nell stopped me, "Joy or Dawn work great. Degreases her and cleans the tub all at once. She may look like an angel, but she can be a dirty one, can't you, Bits?"

"Well," said Bitsy, drawing herself up to her full six-year-old height, "Sometimes Heart and me get dirty playing at the farm. But then Grandmary says, 'Time to get cleaned up before Gramps gets home.' Gramps don't like dirt, do you, Gramps?"

Walter picked her up in a bear hug, "I only like dirt when you're under it." He kissed her cheek and set her down.

Bitsy straightened her shirt and looked up at me from under long lashes, "Aunt Ruthie, do you have any grapes?"

I had forgotten about her Princess requirements. "Oh, I'm sorry, Bits. I don't think I do."

"Oh, that's OK. I'll just eat 'maginary grapes," she said magnanimously.

Jake scoffed. He'd settled down next to Sojo, petting her and pretending not to listen to Bitsy. "Who wants 'maginary grapes? I want real ice cream. Can I, Aunt Ruthie?"

I nodded. "You and Bitsy can both have some as soon as she finishes her bath. Then off to bed with you both."

The promise of ice cream made for a fast Princess Bath. Soon both children were tucked into twin beds in my guest room. They loved the slanted ceiling and dormer windows. "It's just like a castle," Bitsy informed me.

Goodnight kisses and hugs given and received, Walter left us to get himself ready for bed. He had to leave early in the morning for a couple of days of business in Burlington.

Finally, nearly exploding with curiosity, Barb asked Mary Nell for her story. "I must have missed something. I didn't know Jake was coming."

Mary Nell swirled the wine in her glass before taking a sip. "It started with Walter's being stubborn. He had some business to do in Burlington, and he insisted he would drive. He's had a few heart problems lately, and I didn't want him to drive all this way alone. But he hates to feel like I'm babysitting him. So I came up with the idea of bringing Bitsy with us. We could give Betty, her mother, some time off. Betty is great with Bits, but she does take up a lot of space. So I called Ruth to see if we could visit. My purported reason for coming along with Walter.

"Walter agreed. We could show Bits the country, and I could help drive. I told Belle about my plan, and she suggested we bring Jake, too. It would give Bitsy a playmate, give Janie and Win a break, and allow Jake to have some time with his beloved Aunt Ruthie.

"When Belle and I told Janie about our idea, she said she had to ask Jake. He's the one who insisted on the surprise." Mary Nell took another swallow of wine.

"So here we are. And I am still happy to take Bitsy and go to a hotel while Walter's gone. You two really don't have to put us up. You don't even know us." She looked serious. "I mean it."

"I know you do. And I mean this: I want you to stay. Jake and Bitsy will have fun playing with Sojo. We can show you the town. Hell, Barb may even make you search for gold."

Barb laughed, "I just might."

"That sounds intriguing, but I've had it tonight. I'll see y'all in the morning." Mary Nell waggled her fingers over her shoulder as she headed toward Barb's place and her bed.

Walter left early the next morning, before we had had our breakfast. He carried off a cup of coffee saying he would stop for food along the way. Mary Nell extracted promises of being careful and calling her before she walked him to his car and waved as he drove away.

"You two seem to have a great marriage," I remarked. "Rare to see these days."

Mary Nell nodded, "I got very lucky. Walter is my rock. He keeps me steady. He's my home. It scares me to think of him not being with me. He just has to take care of himself." She took a deep breath. "OK, kids, what are we going to do today?"

Jake and Bitsy looked at each other and giggled. "We want to 'splore," Jake declared.

Barb looked up from the stack of papers she seemed to have permanently at hand. "Do you want to explore the cellar with me? I want to look again to see if we can find another message from Josiah Lake, the man who built this house."

"Yes, yes!" shouted Jake.

"Yes, yes!" shouted Bitsy.

"Finish your breakfast and we'll go down below," Barb promised.

Dawdling ceased. Milk was drunk and cereal eaten with alacrity. "OK, Aunt Barb, let's GO!" Jake jumped out of his chair.

"Easy now, Jakester. Mind Aunt Barb," I reminded him.

"We will!" came the chorus as they followed Barb down the dark, twisty stairs into the exciting possibilities of the cellar.

While they explored, Mary Nell and I chatted. It was as if we had known each other for years rather than a few hours. I was in the middle of explaining how Barb and I came to buy the houses when we heard a loud whoop from below.

We hurried downstairs to find Barb sitting on the floor, mouth agape. Jake danced around pumping his fist in the air, and Bitsy arranged a pile of about a dozen small golden nuggets into a circle.

"I found 'em, Aunt Ruthie! Look! Up there!" Jake pointed at a mess of leaves, grass, string, twigs and insulation that sat on top of the sill plate of the stone cellar wall. He had been shining the flashlight along the ceiling when he saw "a big shine."

"So I climbed up on top of that old table and putted my hand in there. And that old chickmunk had put these little gold rocks in there. And when I showed them to Aunt Barb, she said 'Oh, oh, oh!' and sat down in the floor."

I picked him up and hugged him. "I'll bet she did, Jake! You are the hero! You found what Aunt Barb's been looking for!"

Chapter 9 — September 2

Keeping Jake and Bitsy occupied for the rest of their visit was no problem. They wanted to do nothing but " 'splore" and hunt for gold. Barb was happy to be the expedition leader, leaving Mary Nell and me with time to ourselves. At the local brew pub, we discovered a mutual fondness for locally crafted beers and cheeses. We tried many, settling on a double-sharp cheddar and a chocolate stout as our top picks.

When Walter returned from Burlington ready to pack up and head West, I felt my first pang of homesickness since leaving Oklahoma. I wanted to go with them. Jake and I clung to each other – Jake begging me to come see him "sooner than soon." I promised I would.

As they drove away, I felt a tear drip down my cheek. I quickly wiped it away and saw Barb doing the same.

"Those kids really burrowed into my heart," she said sadly. "Do you know what Bitsy said to me this morning? She looked at me seriously, closing her brown eye and squinting with her blue one, and said, 'Aunt Barb? I never had an aunt before. Only Uncle Rusty. Will you still be my aunt when I'm gone?' Isn't that sweet? And Mary Nell said Walter taught her to do that thing with the eyes. He does it, too. Says he sees clearer with his blue eye." She brushed away another tear.

"Good grief, Barb! We need to stop this crap! I've got a bunch of receipts to go through. I'm going to get busy. I suggest you do the same."

"Geez, Ruth," she sighed.

I patted her head as I passed by, "I know."

Within a few minutes, I had receipts spread out around me, double-checking them against my spreadsheet, pretending that this task was important and necessary, when Barb sat down across from me, ever-present stack of papers in her arms. "Why don't you get a briefcase? Or a backpack?" I asked her.

"For what? I don't have a job." Barb said seriously.

"For that giant stack of papers you tote everywhere!"

She seemed to notice them for the first time. "Oh, yeah. You're right. It would be easier. I'll stop and get something. I'm going to CHS. Do a little research."

I pulled my eyebrows together, "What is CHS? And are you sure you can get there? You seem pretty preoccupied."

"Um, yeah. I guess. I've been thinking that maybe I'm wrong about California. I've read dozens and dozens of passenger lists. No Josiah Lake. So I'm going to go do some more reading. Maybe something will occur to me. At CHS. Um, Centerbury Historical Society." She wandered out the door, mumbling to herself.

A very different Barb strode purposefully into my living room a couple of hours later. "I met the most fascinating woman at CHS. She's an historian. She said she can 'read houses,' whatever that means. She's interested in our houses because she says Josiah built a number of important buildings in the area – including the old meeting house that CHS is in. Anyway, she's coming over in an hour. I invited her to tea. And she wants to look at your woodwork."

Well, that was a new one. Nobody had ever wanted to look at my woodwork before. I amused myself for several minutes listing all the other things of mine nobody had ever asked to see.

I did manage to straighten up the table I had strewn with receipts and to run the feather duster over the top of the tables and paneling so that our visitor could see the details of the woodwork unencumbered by spider webs, dog hair, and construction debris.

Barb was pacing when I arrived in her living room. "Sit down," I ordered, "you are making me crazy."

She gave me her exasperated-teacher look, but did sit. "Was it Winnie the Pooh who was always at sixes and sevens?" she asked seriously.

"Barb, I don't know. I haven't read Winnie the Pooh in fifty years. Why are you at sixes and sevens? You were fine when you got back from CHS."

"I'm feeling inept. I'm missing the kids. How could I get so attached to them in such a short time? I can't seem to make a decision. And I think I made a mistake inviting Jane Marple to tea." She sighed heavily.

"Jane Marple? Really? What was her mother thinking? Imagine how terrible it would be to be cast in life as a spinster sleuth in an Agatha Christie novel!" My temperature rose. "It's as bad as naming kids outlandish things like Moon Unit or South West or Krystal Shanda Lear." I snorted in irritation.

"Cool your jets, Ruth. Her name is Janet Maples. I had a tongue slip. Although someone who digs into the history of houses probably is a sleuth of sorts." The corners of her mouth twitched upwards.

Good. My diatribe succeeded in cheering her up. I looked at my watch. "So where is this building dick? I thought she was coming ten minutes ago."

"'Building dick'? Good God, Ruth! What the hell are you thinking?"

"Poor word choice. Sorry. I meant detective. 'Dick' for 'detective', you know, like Raymond Chandler."

Her exasperated look returned. "OK. But PLEASE do not call her a 'dick', building or otherwise."

I was saved by the bell.

Barb returned from answering the door and led the way into the living room. She was followed by Janet, a tiny, drab woman dressed in brown. She had brown eyes encircled by brown glasses. Her brown hair was pulled back into a long brown braid looped around the back of her head. She had a hop in her step, a chirp in her voice, and an unusual way of cocking her head to study what was before her. She wasn't Jane Marple. She was Christopher (or Christine?) Wren.

She moved through the houses picking out particular architectural details, waving her arms and dramatically declaiming all sorts of metaphysical "truths" that she pulled out of the "ley lines" she was certain ran directly through our houses. She mixed in sacred geometry, Native American religious beliefs, something about eugenics and the Abenaki people, and Fibonacci spirals. She sounded impressive, able to pull together references from so many cultural traditions. Until I really listened. Then I knew: I was hearing some of the purest hogwash ever uttered.

Chapter 10 — September 3

I slept poorly the night after the crazy historian's visit. I had bizarre dreams about sacred burial grounds and chambered nautiluses. When Barb came looking for a cup of coffee, I was sitting and staring at the mantle.

"I'm so sorry about yesterday. I will never invite a stranger to tea again," Barb promised.

"I keep thinking there's something there in all that gibberish. I may just go to the hysterical society and do a little research myself."

"Ruth, don't tease. I found her upsetting."

"Come on, Barb. If we don't laugh, we will have to cry. And I truly do want to find out if there's anything to what she said about Abenaki sacred sites. I think that really is the name of the native peoples who lived in Vermont."

"OK. Whatever. But I'm not going back to the CHS without calling first to make sure she's not there."

"You know, when I first saw her yesterday, I thought she looked like a little wren. But I picked the wrong bird. I'm sure she escaped from a Swiss clock. Cuckoo! Cuckoo!"

Barb rolled her eyes, "Ha ha! I am going to forget Janet Maples ever happened." She poured more coffee and strode back to her kitchen where she said she was going to scrub out the refrigerator.

I grabbed a stack of note cards I used for recipes and wrote a word or two at the top of several: Abenaki, Fibonacci, Necromancy, Golden Section, Freemasons. Then iPad in hand, I mounted my investigation.

I Googled, made notes, and followed links for a couple of hours. I found connections and parallels and interesting intersections of information. I jotted down key ideas and links as I found them and soon had a handful of note cards covered in my small writing.

I lay them out on the table and looked for a pattern. Maybe a Tarot layout would work. Or a Canfield spread. I tried both. Nothing clicked.

I remembered my aunt coaxing me into playing 52-card Pickup just before she threw the deck into the air. "Now pick up all 52 of them!" she laughed. Maybe I should try that.

I gathered all my note cards into a stack and had just thrown them ceiling-ward when Barb resurfaced.

"What are you doing?" she asked in surprise as cards floated down all over the room.

"Just looking for a random pattern," I replied nonchalantly.

"Oh, God, not you, too!" Barb drew back in mock horror. "Just give it up, Ruth. It might be too dangerous. Anyway, listen to this. I found something I had forgotten about. Remember that jeweler, Jodie, told us there was gold in Vermont? Maybe Josiah found those nuggets around here."

"Maybe they're the lost treasure of the Abenaki," I said. "Or the Freemasons."

"Stop it!" Barb laughed. "Oh, Ruth, she was funny in a sad way, wasn't she?"

I nodded. "All jokes aside, I think she's right about the Abenaki. There was a horrific eugenics program in Vermont in the 1920s and 30s. The plan was to breed better Vermonters by eliminating any taint from the gene pool: alcoholics, indigents, mental patients, and the Abenaki. They sterilized hundreds. The zoological zealots nearly eradicated the Abenaki. The few who were left had to hide. Or pass as white. If she grew up with that background, it's no wonder she's nuts."

"Maybe. But Ruth, I think you should give it up. You'll end up raving in strangers' living rooms."

"OK. OK. Why don't you go clean more appliances?"

Barb left, shaking her head. I went back to Googling.

Chapter 11 — September 13

For several days after our raving lunatic, or "RL" as Barb had taken to calling her, first materialized in our living room I was obsessed with her ravings. I convinced myself that she did make sense in a crazy way. I continued my diggings, creating more topics, writing more notes. I even had to buy more cards.

I also started mumbling to myself while I was thinking. Once while Barb and I were at the grocery waiting to check out I heard myself say, "The eye over the pyramid is always open." Barb looked at me in concern while the cashier and other shoppers turned away, afraid to be caught staring at the crazy woman.

Actually, that incident scared me. I put aside my note cards and concentrated on working with Sojo. I played games with her in the house, sending her right or left around corners. I moved a trashcan to the middle of the porch and practiced getting her to turn tightly around it. I set up jumps in various configurations and practiced front and rear crosses.

Brenda, my trainer, sent an email announcing "run-thrus" on September 13. Since I had no idea what "run-thrus" were, I didn't initially get excited. Then I called Belle.

"Oh, that's great, Ruth," Belle enthused. She doesn't easily enthuse. I was unprepared for it.

"Why?" I asked.

"Because it's a mock trial. You can practice a full run in a non-threatening environment," she explained.

"That sounds pretty threatening to me. What do I need to take?"

"Dog, crate, leash, water, treats. Normal stuff."

"Why do I need a crate? All I have is the big wire one she sleeps in. It's heavy. Do I really need to take it?"

"Yes. You have to have a place to put Sojo while you walk the course. You know about walking the course, don't you?"

"Um, walk around and look for the numbers to see where to steer Sojo."

"Well, yes," Belle said, "but you also need to figure out how you're going to run it. Will you lead out or do a running start? Do you put her on your left or on your right? Will you use a front cross or a rear? You need to practice how you'll move, where you'll stop, what you'll say. It's a very important skill to learn."

"OK. How long will I have? That seems like a lot to do." I was getting more nervous now.

"Eight minutes, generally. You'll get a course map before the walk. Study it. Look at the flow of the course. Then when you get to walk, you'll have a head start."

"Oh, Belle. I don't think I should even go. I don't know how to do all that stuff!" I was getting close to full-blown panic.

"Bull crap! Of course you should go. It's the perfect way to learn. If you don't know what to do, ask Brenda. Or ask anyone. Agility people are always willing to help. Remember that although most agility folks are very competitive, we're not competing against each other as much as against ourselves. It's not a zero-sum game where for me to win you have to lose. We both can win! I think that's why we all help each other so much."

"OK, OK. I'll ask questions. I'll look at the map and walk around the field. Then what?"

"Then they'll call your name and you will enter the ring, take Sojo off her leash, and run the course you just walked only this time with Sojo. Then you put her back on her leash, leave the ring, and give her treats."

"Well that sounds easy," I said with an eye roll.

Belle ignored my sarcasm, "It is. You'll love it. Call me when you get home from Brenda's." And she hung up. No goodbye, no good luck, no break a leg. She left it up to just me and Sojo.

I arrived at Brenda's field early, of course—I'm always early—with Sojo and paraphernalia. I wasn't the first to arrive, thank God, so I could study what to do: sign in, get the course map, set up the crate, put Sojo in it, mingle.

As I mingled, I realized Belle forgot to tell me one important item to bring, a chair. I guess I'd sit on the ground. Then I noticed a woman in my class comfortably sitting in a canvas chair next to her light-weight canvas crate on a large dirt-covering mat. Ah! I guess Belle forgot to tell me several things I needed to buy.

I studied the course map, trying to figure out what it told me. My classmate noticed my confusion and offered to help. She showed me how to read it, following the numbers, and how to plan my course with it. She even drew my path on the map for me. I decided that as complex as this appeared, I'd probably better add an astrolabe to my purchase list. Maybe Celestial Navigation would improve my chances.

Then Brenda said loudly that the course was open for walking. I joined dozens of mental patients wandering through the dog obstacles, swinging their arms and saying "Jump" or "Tunnel" under their breaths. It took me a minute to realize that they were practicing their runs sans dogs, and that I was supposed to do the same.

First I had to find those damned numbers. I looked at the map in my hand again. It bore no relationship to the layout of the ring in front of me. Then someone yelled, "Number 1 is over here." Ah, I was in the wrong corner. Oh, God, help me get through this.

My next thought was that I would watch where everyone else went then follow them. But the problem was that not everyone did the same thing. Some walked to the left of the second jump and some walked to the right. Some did front crosses and some did rear. I even saw someone do some sort of move that would have put the dog behind her! I thought, "At least I don't have to worry about that. I am NEVER going to be in front of Sojo.

I decided just to jump in. I walked past the first few obstacles, pointing at them and mumbling the commands. Then I got to a spot where I had no idea how I could get to the next obstacle without jumping the jump myself.

The friendly classmate, whose name I have since discovered was Ann, came to my rescue. She said, "If you can't get where you need to be from where you are, you need to be somewhere else." I looked at her blankly. She laughed and said, "Maybe you could back into it. You need to be next to that tunnel to get her through those last three jumps. Right?" I nodded, unable to come up with words. "Then how can you get her through this jump and the teeter and wind up at that tunnel?"

The light dawned. I needed to put Sojo on my right not my left. And I could do that with a cross. I sucked in a ragged breath, croaked "Thanks," and started back at the prior obstacle, taking a new path forward and getting where I needed to be. Success!

Finally the game started. I watched people with small dogs start the runs, jumping bars only four inches off the ground. Some were successful, many not. Dogs would knock down bars they tried to jump, leap sideways off the teeter-totter, or get the "zoomies" and tear all over the field as fast as they could go while their handlers helplessly called "Come! Come!"

All the jumps were raised, and the next group of dogs ran. Sojo was in the fourth group since she jumps sixteen inches. Finally, my turn came. I put Sojo in a stay and walked toward the first jump. I took a deep breath, said, "OK, Sojo, come jump." And she rocketed forward. I successfully navigated her through two jumps, a tunnel, the A-frame and another jump when I got lost. I was so worried about getting to the right side of the tunnel, I couldn't remember where to go next. And, although I could see the numbers of the nearby obstacles, I couldn't remember the number of the last jump we'd taken.

I stopped. Sojo came to me, yipped, circled me, and spun in front of me. I was mortified.

From across the field, Brenda shouted, "Number 6. Table."

I smiled in relief and directed Sojo to lie down on the table. While she did that, I took a look around, quickly recalculated my course, took a deep breath, and called Sojo to the dogwalk, the canine balance beam. The rest of the run was fine.

When Sojo crossed the finish line, everyone cheered. Brenda called, "Nice, Ruth! Your virgin run is over! The longest seventy-five seconds of your life."

Seventy-five seconds! I could swear it was at least ten minutes.

Sojo and I celebrated on the sidelines. She ate her fancy salmon treats and I danced with her. We did it!

When I got home, I gave a summary of our activities to Barb then called Belle to deliver the play-by-play.

"That's wonderful, Ruth. She stayed with you, took every obstacle, and you recovered. Bravo!"

Belle surprised me with her praise. "Oh, um, thanks," I stuttered. I had expected to be scolded about getting lost.

After I hung up, I collapsed in my recliner next to the fireplace. My seventy-five second adrenaline rush had worn me out. Suddenly, Sojo jumped up from her place on the floor beside me and barked madly at the old beehive oven next to the fireplace. I looked in it just in time to see a striped tail slip between two bricks.

"There's a chipmunk in the oven," I yelled, hoping Barb would hear. I grabbed a flashlight and a poker and knelt in front of the little oven. I jabbed at the crack where the chipmunk had disappeared until the crack widened.

In order to see further into the small domed brick oven, I had to practically crawl inside it. Once there with the flashlight in hand, I could see that the crack I had widened was next to an iron plate built into the sidewall. I stuck my head in farther, trying to see better, when Barb nearly caused a concussion.

"Wrong kind of oven for suicide," she announced loudly.

I startled, knocking my head on the brick oven ceiling, thrusting out my flashlight to catch myself, and swearing loudly first because of the knot on my forehead and then for what I saw.

Holding the flashlight with one hand, I was able to slowly pull the plate away from the wall. It was hinged on one side. In fact, it wasn't a plate at all. It was a door to a box set into the wall of the oven. I felt around inside the opening until I touched something cold and rather rough. Hesitantly and with no small measure of trepidation, I slid my finding out of the hole.

In the light we could see it was a tobacco box, like the 1860 Old Virginia Smoke box Barb had found when it fell from the chimney in the cellar. But this one was rustier and looked charred. Barb fetched the penetrating oil while I wiped away some of the grime so that I could get a better hold as I tried to prize open the lid. My first attempt resulted in my squirting the box through my hands and across the room.

The next attempt, using paper towels and judiciously applied oil, I eased the top up, bit by bit, until it finally opened.

"Hurry the hell up!" Barb commanded with uncharacteristic impatience. "What is in it?"

"Nothing I can see," I said as I turned the box upside down and tapped the bottom. A little rust sifted onto the hearth stone where I worked. Next I held it over my upturned palm and tapped the bottom again. This time I felt something soft touch my skin. Turning it over and peering inside again, I saw that what I had originally taken to be the painted inside of the box was actually a piece of paper, tightly pushed against the sides until it was nearly invisible. I shimmied it up and down, loosening it from the rust that held it, and finally got a hold on it when it extended about a half -inch beyond the metal box.

The paper was yellowed and very brittle, and covered in typeset print. "It's a page from a book or something," I not very helpfully informed Barb. I smoothed it carefully onto the table beside my chair as Barb turned on the light. We could then see that the page contained an article from a newspaper although it was missing a date or title. It started mid-sentence and described a new sleigh design that provided better maneuverability in deep snow.

"Damn!" Barb exclaimed. "It's just packing for whatever was in the box."

I stared at the clipping for a few seconds before an idea finally dawned. I blame my slowness on my adrenaline overdose earlier that day. When I turned the clipping over, we could see an entire article from the Centerbury Clarion, dated May 19, 1861.

LOCAL JOINER RETURNS TO CENTERBURY
by Jeremiah Lake

After four years absence, master joiner and house-wright Josiah Lake has returned to Centerbury to take up his trade. When asked by this reporter whether he had come home after making his fortune, Mr. Lake merely raised an eyebrow and said, "I lost one but found another." No amount of prodding could produce further illumination of his cryptic remarks.

"Well this is just swell," Barb groused. "We already knew he'd been gone for four years. I want to know where the hell he was. And what does that coy remark about finding one fortune but losing another mean?"

I looked at her seriously. "I think, Barbara King, that's what you are meant to discover."

Chapter 12 — September 28

About ten days ago I learned of a real agility trial coming up in mid-October. The entries hadn't closed, so with the long-distance encouragement of Belle, I filled out my entry form and mailed it in.

Then I panicked.

Sally called me the following day, "Congratulations, kiddo. I hear Belle convinced you to enter a real trial. I didn't think you'd be able to withstand her full-court press."

"She can be very pushy," I replied.

"Oh, Ruth, you do not know the half of it!" Sally cackled. "But anyway, I'm tickled you entered. Just go into it with the idea of playing with your dog, and don't get all hung up on Q'ing or winning. To misquote Hamlet, 'The play's the thing.' It's about having a good time and challenging yourself. 'Just do it', as those shoe people say."

"Well, aren't you just full of quotes! I guess I will do it, Sal. I mailed the entry. But I am a little nervous about it."

"A little nervous won't hurt you. If you get scared spitless, that's a different story. Then you have to meditate and drink a lot of wine. That's what cures my nerves."

"Oh, Sally, I have never seen you nervous."

"See?" she cackled. "On another topic, how's Barb? She making any progress in finding out where that gold came from? Boy, you two sure made Jake happy. He hasn't shut up yet about finding gold in the 'chickmunk's' nest in Aunt Barb's cellar."

"Aunt Barb has been buried in historical documents. She's now decided that Josiah Lake got the gold in Vermont during the little gold rush here. But did you hear about the box I found in the fireplace?"

"Yep, Belle told me. What have you made of that?"

"I have no idea why anyone would hide a newspaper clipping inside a tobacco box in a strongbox inside an oven," I snipped. "Sorry, Sally. I'm just exasperated. I have no notion, however farfetched, that would explain it. How about you? Any great ideas?"

"Hmm. Let me think. Maybe the can contained something else that was wrapped in the newspaper so it wouldn't get broken or it wouldn't rattle. And someone stole it. Maybe the gold. Maybe the chipmunks took it and put it in their nest." She was on a roll, picking up speed with each idea. "Of course the chipmunks would need help getting the box open. Oh, I know. I bet it was a gypsy. Or a pirate. Probably a pirate."

"Sally, have you been at that wine?"

"Of course not. I'm just playing. Dreaming up solutions is really fun. You two should try it. Maybe by being outlandish you'll actually come up with something."

When Barb came by about an hour later, I told her about Sally's suggested activity. "What a great idea!" she enthused. "Let's try it."

"OK. Why don't we each go off and think up outlandish ideas. Then we can go over them together."

Barb rolled her eyes, "Ruth, don't be such a…such a poop."

"A poop?"

"Yes. A party poop." She looked at me with concern. "Have you forgotten how to play?"

"You're the second person today to tell me I need to play. I thought I played fine." I felt a little hurt by this turn in the conversation. Of course I played. I played with Sojo, when I wasn't training her. Well, sometimes I did. "OK, but I can't do it right now. I have to go train, er, play with Sojo." I called Sojo and went out the back door with her, calling over my shoulder, "I'll be over to play with you in about an hour."

Our backyard was spectacularly beautiful at the end of September. Several of the large maples had turned incredible shades of orange and scarlet. The green grass, blue sky and blazing trees halted me in delight for a few minutes before I went looking for Sojo's ball.

She saw me looking for it and found it first, brought it to me, and dropped it at my feet. I picked it up and tossed it directly to her. She caught it then crowed in pleasure, "Roo-roo-roo!"

I had never heard her do that before. I wondered if it was a fluke. I tossed her the ball again, she caught it and roo-roo'ed with even more emphasis.

By now I was laughing out loud. I tossed the ball further out. She didn't catch it, but fetched it without crowing. Then I put her in a stay, backed up about twenty feet, and pitched it underhand to her. She caught it with a hop and roo-roo'ed all the way back to me.

So. She did know the difference. She only crowed when she caught the ball.

I tried several other variations, sometimes with her catching the ball in a highflying leap and sometimes missing it. She invariably crowed with success and remained silent when she missed. And she crowed longest and loudest with a tricky catch.

By now, I was so proud of my dog I was crowing as I called her inside and went to tell Barb.

Lying on her sofa with her feet propped on pillows and a thin, bright scarf covering her face was my old friend. She was so still I thought she was dead. "What the hell are you doing?" I demanded.

She startled, sat up, and said dreamily, "Oh, Ruth, you should try it. It feels wonderful."

"What's so wonderful about scaring your friend half to death. You looked like a corpse."

"I was reversing the blood flow from my feet. It really does feel good."

"So why the cloth on your face?"

"Oh," she chuckled. "The light was in my eyes, and the scarf was on the back of the couch. And it felt good rising and falling across my cheeks with each breath."

"Well, OK. But try not to look dead in the future."

"Oh, Ruth," she said softly, shaking her head. "Are you ready to brainstorm?"

"No. Not yet. I've come to tell you about Sojo." I described Sojo's crowing and offered to let Barb see for herself.

She rose from the couch languidly. "Show me." She glided to the back door.

"Sojo, let's go play ball and show this boneless specter how you can crow." I turned back to Barb, "Are you sure you are all right? You are acting very strange."

"I'm fine. Just feeling very loose. Show me the wonder dog," she said leaning against the back wall.

Sojo and I played for a few minutes with the same results as before. After her third or fourth crowing, Barb got tickled and laughed herself back to normalcy. She was still chuckling when she sat back down on her couch. "From now on," she proclaimed, "I'll use Sojo as my preferred mood-altering substance."

"What did you use before?" I asked suspiciously.

She raised an eyebrow and shook her head slightly. "Let's brainstorm."

An hour or so later we had come up with a raft of silliness and one idea worth exploring. Barb had discovered in her research that Centerbury had at least one well-known abolitionist resident: Lucinda Dodd. Mrs. Dodd was credited with helping dozens of escaped slaves find their way to the safety of Canada.

Letters of introduction and safe-passage were often carried by the runaways from one stop to the next so that the next "station master" along the way would not need to fear being tricked by slave hunters hungry to capture their quarry.

Barb suggested that the can with a clipping about Josiah Lake in it would serve the same purpose as a letter. It could be a ticket on the Underground Railroad.

I was surprised that once Barb came up with the idea we were able to flesh it out into a plausible explanation. "Sally was right," I conceded. "Now how do we prove we're right?"

"I am wondering if there could be a secret room tucked in around this big fireplace. Look at the size of it. It's about six feet by ten feet. Not all of that space can be chimney. And I hate to say it, but I think I am going to get in touch with the Raving Lunatic. She may be crazy as a quilt, but she does know something about the architecture of these old houses."

"Oh, no!" I moaned. "Not the cuckoo bird! Don't you know anyone else?"

Barb shook her head sadly. "Janet Maples is it."

Chapter 13 — October 7

I woke up with a sense of gloom on this sunny, crisp day that had nothing gloomy about it. It was my sixty-first birthday. I hadn't told anyone. I didn't want to acknowledge it.

When I checked my email I had no good wishes from anyone. Just the same old political solicitations for money and spam asking me if I wanted to enlarge my penis. I had thought that someone might remember.

I spent the next hour examining myself in the mirror — short light brown hair with silver temples and sideburns, freckle-sprinkled nose, gray-green eyes behind tri-focals, aunt's droopy eyelids, father's hanging jowls, mother's thick double chin. The older I get the more I look like my old relatives. Or maybe all old people have droopy eyelids and hanging jowls. I was not ready to admit to being a part of "old people" yet despite the fact that I was now officially over sixty.

I was still examining myself, having moved on to hands and arms, when Barb came in. "Raving Lunatic is still out of town," she informed me. "Won't be back for a couple of weeks."

"That's a relief," I replied as I continued to look at myself in the living room mirror.

After a few seconds of puzzled silence, Barb asked, "What in the hell are you doing?"

"Oh, just examining the evidence," I sighed.

"Evidence of what?"

"Time's wreckage," my flair for the melodramatic flared.

Barb moved beside me and peered around my left shoulder to see the mirror. "Oh, I don't know. We don't look too bad for a couple of old broads," she grinned. "We still have our hair and most of our teeth. No nose warts. No long black hairs sprouting from our chins. Boobs still above our waists. Not too bad."

I swatted at her. "Let me grieve my lost youth in peace." I picked up a photo I had found earlier and handed it to her. It showed two young women laughing into a mirror. Each was wearing a bright pink headband holding a tall pink feather, a bright pink dress belted low and skirted short, fishnet stockings and bare feet. Their reflected faces were rouged, smooth, and full of mischief.

"Oh, my God, Ruthie! It's from Rush Week our senior year. Look at us! We are so young. And so thin!" She looked from photo to mirror and back. "Look, we're in the same pose forty years later." She left the mirror and moved to the window where scarlet and gold sugar maples filled the small, wavy panes.

After standing at the window for a couple of minutes. Barb turned back to me. With two determined strides, she was back at my side giving me a one-armed hug around the waist. "I got to feeling a little nostalgic myself about our loss of fresh-faced eagerness," she waved the photo toward me, "until I looked out the window." She turned me around until I was facing the way she'd come.

"Look at that again," she ordered as she handed me the photo. "Those girls were sap-green, newly furled leaflets. But these blazing beauties," she swept her arm toward the maples out the window, "have been around a while. And they are flaunting their age with wild abandon. Nobody can look at them and say 'Poor old things. Past their prime.' They are glorying in their prime!"

"And by extension, we should, too, huh?" I asked quietly.

Barb nodded with a familiar mischievous glint. "So how about we go glory? Let's spend the day with the brazen hussies. Let's be leaf peepers!"

I quickly dug through my basket of tourist brochures I'd collected for future adventures. I pulled out a bright orange and red pamphlet entitled "Best Leaf Peeping Trails," and flipped it open. "According to this, every road in Vermont is a prime spot for seeing fall color. So let's just be Vermont tourists for the day.

We can drive around and stop for photos or snacks or walking Sojo. It's cool enough to take her."

Barb agreed, "Let's make a big loop. You pick the route. I'll be ready in fifteen minutes."

For the next five or six hours we drove through southern Vermont. We drove on four-lane highways where we saw wide-open vistas with layers of tapestried mountains and on one- lane tracks through national forests where single trees called "Look at me!" We passed through towns with colonial houses encircled by maples set aflame by autumn's arrival and tiny villages whose white-steepled churches glowed against bright blue skies. We fell in love with all we saw.

We stopped frequently for photos but none captured the immensity of the views or intensity of the hues. We bought apple cider and pie at farm stands and cheese and maple-flavored cookies at general stores. We bought pumpkins and bittersweet and gathered boughs of maple and birch.

When we arrived home we were sated with autumn's abundance. We had told each other, "Oh, look at that!" so many times that Barb christened this our Oh Look Day.

I had an idea about creating prose postcards to send to friends and begged off when Barb invited me in for coffee. She insisted that I come inside for a few minutes after I walked Sojo. She said she had something to show me. I sighed, loudly, and agreed but stipulated that it was for only a very few minutes.

When Sojo and I finished our successful circumnavigation of the back yard and walked into Barb's kitchen, it was dark. "Where are you?" I yelled.

"Living room," she replied.

I opened the door and stepped into a party. Balloons floated against the ceiling; a huge cake sat on the dining room table; Jack and Ted were passing plates to a few people sitting in the living room. Everyone shouted, "Happy Birthday!"

I was gob-smacked. As I stood stock-still peering around in amazement, a small body crashed into my legs and hugged my waist.

"Did we 'prize you, Aunt Ruthie?" Jake, curls tumbling and eyes snapping, jumped up and down in delight.

"You sure did, Jakey!" I bent to hug him properly and look over his shoulder as I did, hoping to see who else was here. My niece, Janie, and her new husband, the gentle giant, Win, stepped into my line of sight as they came forward for hugs. Belle, Sally and Jo Murphy, a high school friend I'd reconnected with in Plainview, were beaming on the couch.

I sat down heavily in a nearby chair, unable to trust my legs any longer. Jake said excitedly, "You look just like Aunt Barb did when I finded the gold in the chickmunk's bed! Are you going to say 'Oh, oh, oh!' too?"

I put my hands on my cheeks and said, "Oh, oh, oh!"

Everyone laughed and gathered around, talking at once. Despite my surprise-induced shock and the general cacophony of my friends and family, I was able to patch together an explanation for their appearance.

I had forgotten that Jo and I shared a birthday, but she hadn't. When she told Belle and Sally that she thought it would be fun to spend our birthday together, they launched Operation Vermont Birthday. They convinced Janie and Win to join them, and the six of them had flown in that morning. Barb's maneuvering to spend the day leaf-peeping had left the house free for party decorating.

I was still reeling, having difficulty comprehending the sequence of events, but I could drink, and Jack and Ted kept my glass filled with cold, crisp Sauvignon Blanc while Jake entertained a waggley Sojo.

I raised a glass to wish Jo a happy birthday and teased her that at least she got something special with her sixty-second birthday – Social Security. All I got was older.

We ate, drank, talked, laughed, and had an altogether splendid party. When everyone finally adjourned to their appointed bedrooms, Barb and I walked outside with Sojo.

"That was absolutely the most wonderful birthday of my life!" I told her with a hug.

She bent and picked up a bright red maple leaf, "We can thank these brazen hussies for reminding us how to glory."

I nodded and smiled, "Glory be!"

Chapter 14 — October 8

The next morning was less glorious—six extra people in the house and no hot water. The first to notice was Win, always an early riser, who wandered into the kitchen wearing only a frilly bathrobe tied around his waist. I was pouring my first cup of coffee.

"I like the skirt," I told him.

A flush crept up his neck, "I forgot my robe. This is Janie's." He backed toward the coffeepot keeping his bare backside pointed away from me.

"Forget your pants, too?" I asked.

"Mmm, no. I'm just waiting for the water to warm up for a shower and I smelled coffee."

"How long have you been waiting?" I felt a niggle of dread.

"About five minutes, I think."

"Well, that's a problem. We always get plenty of hot water in under a minute. I'll see if one of the guys will look at it." I headed out the door to the garage where the carpenters and painters, the "guys", had set up shop for the past three months.

"Hey, Tommy, could you take a look at the boiler? We don't have any hot water."

"Sure, Ruth. I'd be happy to. I'll do it right now." He flashed his charmer's smile as he climbed down from the scaffolding flanking the garage doors. He moved like a spider monkey with agility, grace, and strength.

It had been pleasant watching these young men work, clambering on our roofs, balancing on the scaffolds. Jack and Ted thought so, too. They dropped by nearly every day to "check on progress." Barb and I suspected they were much more interested in watching the workers. They turned up for their daily progress check just as Tommy returned from the cellar.

"Bad news, Ruth." Tommy's big brown eyes had a left-behind cocker spaniel look. "There's something wrong with the hot water loop off the boiler. I think you need to call a plumber."

"Great," I muttered. Then louder, "Does anyone know a good plumber?"

Ted stepped forward holding his cell phone in front of him, "I do, I do! Name's Ray Black. He's good."

He followed me into the kitchen now filled with four women and Win, backed into a corner. I said hello and hurried to the laundry room where I snagged a bath towel for Win.

I wished for my camera. Big, tall, gentle Win, blushing furiously in his frilly loincloth. I tossed him the towel, "Here, toots, wrap up."

He caught the towel one handed and quickly wrapped it around his waist. "What's the story on hot water?"

"Sorry, guy. You're going to have to stink. I have to call the plumber."

Win hurried upstairs to get dressed while I dialed the number Ted read from his phone. Miraculously, Ray Black answered the phone and promised to come over late that afternoon.

I relayed the news to the breakfasters. Jo had used her short-order cook skills and stepped into the void I'd left while dealing with the hot water problem. "Sorry, Jo. Busman's holidays are no fun. I didn't mean for you to have to cook." I told Barb, "Jo's diner is the only decent place to eat within 30 miles of Plainview."

"It's the ONLY place to eat within 30 miles," Jo laughed.

"Nobody can stand the competition," Sally added.

"So, Ruth, what do you want to eat? There are still some eggs left. How about a bacon scramble and toast?"

"Perfect. You are wonderful! Thank you." I glanced around the kitchen where everyone but Win and Jake were present. "Where's Jake?"

Janie, my high-energy niece and Jake's mother, said, "There's a dog in this house. Where do you think he is?"

Just then, a bark sounded from the back yard. "Ah, playing ball." I took a bite of my excellent scramble then asked, "So gang, what does everyone want to do today? I'm free until late afternoon. Barb, can you be a tour guide?" She nodded.

For the next fifteen minutes everyone talked at once. Suggestions were offered and rejected. Eventually it shook out to three separate adventures. Janie, Win, Jake, and Sojo were going to follow the same loop Barb and I had taken yesterday, and stop at a lake for a picnic and playtime.

Barb would drive Jo to Montpelier where Jo wanted to check out the New England Culinary Institute. She was thinking about opening a cooking school and wanted to look at one of the best.

That left Sally, Belle, and me. We decided to go to Saratoga Springs where they wanted to check out a canine performance center, see how it was constructed and whether they could adapt it for Oklahoma summers.

We took our time driving to Saratoga Springs. We found Kodak Moments at every turn. Sally had a new camera that she insisted on using to capture every brightly colored leaf along the way, or so Belle observed.

After Belle and Sally finished their meeting with the owner of the performance center, asking her dozens of questions, we stopped for lunch in the Spa Town, Saratoga Springs. Racing season was over but the streets were still filled with tourists soaking up the sun in outdoor cafes and on park benches.

"What a charming city," Sally said several times, as Belle reminded her. They did agree that they wanted to come back during racing season so they could bet on the ponies.

"I don't know why you even bother betting," Sally scoffed. "You only bet on one horse per race."

"At least I don't lose my shirt," Belle replied.

"Never win anything, either. Did I tell you, Ruth, that I won $1200 on a tri-fecta last spring?" Sally bragged. She turned to Belle, "And don't ask how much I lost. That's not the point."

The drive home seemed very short as Belle and Sally teased each other with sharp tongues and dry wit. I was sore from laughing by the time I pulled into my driveway.

A bright yellow van pulled in behind me. "The plumber, I presume," I announced as I went to meet him.

He was about my age with mostly brown hair and a sun-wrinkled face. He looked around the house as I led him to the cellar door. "I love these old colonials. But they can be damned expensive."

I agreed. We'd already spent more than the annual budget of a small country. And it looked like we were about to spend some more. I followed him into the cellar where he said he could jury-rig the hot water loop for the night, to give us a little hot water for dish washing. And he could put in a new electric tank tomorrow morning. Win would be glad. He hated to miss his shower.

During dinner everyone recounted the day's exploits. Janie and Win had stumbled on a gallery that specialized in illustrations for children's books, Janie's specialty. The gallery owner asked her to send her e-portfolio for consideration for a show next summer. Jo had half a notebook filled with ideas for a small cooking school geared to the Mom & Pop café market. Belle and Sally described the canine performance center and how they might be able to use such a building in their business.

I suddenly realized that Jake was missing. Sojo and I went to find him just moments before I heard him calling from the living room.

"Aunt Ruthie! Aunt Barb! Come see!" He was on the floor, next to the left corner of the fireplace, with lampblack smudges on his face and hands. Beside him, under the beehive oven, a small door was standing open.

"How did you get that door open?" I asked. The door was about twelve inches by fourteen inches and covered on the outside with what looked like very thin brick. When closed, it disappeared into the overall pattern of the brick work.

Jake pointed at the beehive oven. "I stuck my head in that hole and I finded a little door inside. I pushed on that little door and it opened. Then I pushed on the rock by the door and this door by the floor popped open and hitted me in the leg."

Barb reached into the newly revealed opening and felt around. "There's a handle on the left wall. I can't get it to move."

Win knelt beside Barb. "Here, let me try." His large hand disappeared into the hidden recess and a moment later we heard the squawk of wood rubbing against wood. "It's starting to move," he announced. Then with a loud moan, the wall to the left of the fireplace creaked and a section of the paneling opened slightly, revealing yet another door. With another grunt from Win, the door swung open.

"Thank God!" Barb sighed. "We won't need the Raving Lunatic!"

Chapter 15 — October 9

After the discovery of the secret room, none of us could settle down for bed. Speculations about its use, the wildest coming from Win, kept us entertained until Janie noticed that Jake and Sojo had curled up in the corner and fallen asleep.

Everyone went to bed but Jo and me. We finally had a chance to catch up with each other.

"So, you like it here, Ruth? Really? I think I'd have trouble with the cold winters, but after all those years in Chicago, I guess you got acclimated."

"You know, I had more trouble with Oklahoma's never-ending heat than I have ever had with cold. And yes, I do like it here. Very much. It's been fun to reconnect with Barb, and after all the intervening years, find that we are still the same people after all."

"Then there's the politics. I wonder how it would feel to live where the majority agreed with me. I bet my anger levels would be lower."

I smiled, "It's pretty nice when the only letters I write to my senators and congressman are to thank them. But I miss Janie and Jake, and Win. And of course you and Sally and Belle. I can't tell you how excited I was to see you all here. What a surprise!"

"It made a nice birthday present for me, too." Jo said. "As you know, I've been trying to dig myself out of a rut by changing my hair, clothes, name, and even thinking of opening a cooking school. I just feel so stuck. Even Ellen's moving to Plainview didn't help. Now I feel responsible for my sister's happiness, too. I wanted to see how you were doing in a new environment so I could try to picture myself in one."

"Oh, move up here! It would be great! There's a cute little house for sale just around the corner. I'll show you tomorrow. Oh, Jo! I would love it!"

"It was such a stroke of luck running into you in Plainview after not seeing you for 40-something years. I hate to think of losing you again." Jo said. "But selling everything, the diner, the house, and moving here is a bigger change than I think I could handle."

"Then do it in stages. Rent a place here for a few months and see how you like it. Hey, where's Ellen living?"

"She's still in that little apartment Belle and Sally have at BellWhether. Why?"

"Couldn't she live in your house while you're gone? Then you wouldn't have to worry about it. And couldn't Gerry run the diner for you?"

Jo pursed her lips and chewed on the bottom one as she thought. "I don't know about Gerry. She's trying to write, and I imagine she could use some extra money. But if she worked at the diner full-time, I don't think she'd have enough time to write. I'll have to think this through."

"How about Ellen at the diner, helping Gerry?" I suggested.

"Hmm. That's an idea. Oh, Ruth, you've got my wheels turning. I need to think. I have to go to bed." She leaned over me for a hug as she headed up to bed. "I hope I can get to sleep. Goodnight!" She staggered off to bed, her mind clearly detached from her physical activity.

The next morning, we awakened to loud banging on the pipes in the cellar. Ray Black was busily working to restore our household to good odor by providing hot water for bathing early and plentifully.

He succeeded by about ten o'clock, at which time there was a mad dash to the showers. All except Jake and Sojo seemed intent on washing off as much Vermont dust as possible.

Jake, on the other hand, was busy collecting it. Running through the backyard chasing Sojo and rolling in the grass with her, he picked up enough microbes to supply a high school biology class.

When not bathing or eating, everyone continued to expound on their theories about the use of the secret room. Of course, Barb's Underground Railroad explanation seemed the most plausible, but that didn't prevent Win from wild surmises, including the locking away of a wicked first wife/step-mother/crazy aunt.

Sally had the most practical idea—she declared that we needed to photograph and measure the room, noting everything about the physical description in a "straightforward factual style."

"Yes, Detective O'Neill," Belle said meekly while giving Sally a mischievous grin. "Did you all know that Sally was a detective in the Ford County, Kansas Sheriff's Department back in antediluvian times."

I remembered hearing that and how Sally's being shot in the knee had ended that career and left her with a permanent limp. "Good idea, Sally. I'll find a notebook."

Then while I fixed lunch and Jo looked at the Realtor.Com listings for Centerbury, Sally, Win and Barb compiled a comprehensive description of the musty, dusty room beside the chimney. It was, as Barb had speculated earlier, an area of about six feet by ten feet into which the chimney extended about three feet by four feet at the middle of the right wall. Win said that forty-eight square feet wasn't much room, especially since it was only about five feet high, but there was room for someone to lie down.

Sally agreed. "About the size of a jail cell," she said.

As we ate lunch, everyone argued about what to do next. Barb declared that she didn't care what anyone else did, but she was going to take the specs of the secret room to the historical society to see if anyone there had any explanations.

Just then a loud "Roo-roo-roo" sounded from the living room. I jumped up to see what got Sojo going but Jake beat me to the living room.

"Oh, Oh, Oh! Look Aunt Ruthie!" Jake pointed into the secret room where Sojo was pawing at the wall. A brick had come loose at the corner of the chimney, and Sojo dug at it to pull it away from the rest. Each time the brick moved, Sojo celebrated with a crow. She continued to dig and nose at the brick, until it reached a point where she couldn't move it.

By then, the others had come in to listen to Sojo's concert. Sally nudged Belle, "Is she a direct descendent?"

Belle nodded. "But I didn't know she crowed."

I looked up, distracted from Sojo's continued attempts to dig out the brick. "Oh, she just started that. Pretty cute, huh?"

Sally said, "My Dillon was the first dog I ever heard do that. Sojo's his descendent. He'd be about 50 if he were still alive. From the first litter Belle and I ever bred." A tear welled in her eye.

Belle patted the shoulder of her old friend. "None of that, Sal. Dillon was just the first of an amazing number of dogs we've bred, owned and loved. And I'm delighted that Sojo has inherited Dillon's vocal talents. But now let's see what she's crowing about."

Janie, small and agile, crawled into the room and wiggled the brick that Sojo had loosened. Jake tried to help but Janie shooed him away, "I don't want you to mash your fingers, buddy," she told him.

After several minutes of wiggling, she got the brick out far enough to place a small pry behind it. Win saw the chance to help and passed her a long-handled screwdriver. The sweet smile she gave back to him reminded me of what a short time they'd been married.

At last, Janie wedged the brick totally out of the chimney and shined a flashlight, also helpfully supplied by Win, into the exposed opening. "Huh!" she said as she slid the screwdriver into the edge of the hole and pushed out another tobacco tin, of exactly the same brand and age as the other two we'd found.

Barb insisted that we take the tobacco tin into the kitchen where the light was better. She tried to prize the lid off as we had done with the other two. This one was even more stubborn and took the combined efforts of Barb, penetrating oil, and Win's large hand before the rusty top edged off.

Barb shook out petrified mouse turds, at least I hope they were petrified, and a small skeleton key tied with a faded red ribbon. And like the last box, this one was lined with an old newspaper clipping. Barb spread it out on the table in front of us.

The article, like the last, was from the Centerbury Clarion. It was published July 1, 1861, a few weeks after the first, and was written by the same Jeremiah Lake.

LOCAL JOINER FINDS TREASURE MAP

by Jeremiah Lake

Master joiner, Josiah Lake, who only returned to Centerbury last month after an extended absence, has astounded the village trustees by displaying at yesterday's council meeting a map he purports to be of the Centerbury Churchyard. The map, aged and faded, shows a specific spot, marked by a large red X, where Mr. Lake asserts a treasure is buried, most probably in a coffin. His attendance at the trustee meeting was specifically to petition the members for permission to exhume the coffin of Jubulon Asher, which Mr. Lake asserts is located at the X.

When questioned about how he had obtained the map and why he thought it referred to the Centerbury Churchyard, Mr. Lake merely insisted that everyone could see for themselves if they would just let him dig.

The trustees proposed to take the request under advisement and report their decision within the week. Meanwhile, Mr. Lake was advised not to take it upon himself to dig in the churchyard or he would find himself charged with vandalism.

One of the trustees was heard to remark that given Josiah's proclivity for pranks, this map was most likely an elaborate hoax.

The article put a dent in the plans we'd made, but after stewing for a few minutes, Janie and Win decided to go on to Quechee Gorge with Jake and Sojo as they had planned. Belle, Sally, Jo and I were going to drive around the area looking at available real estate. And Barb was going to the historical society hoping to find subsequent articles about Josiah and the treasure.

She said, as she headed out the door, "God, I just hope I don't run into the Raving Lunatic while I'm there."

Vain hope.

That evening Win and Janie cooked dinner while the rest of us sipped wine and listened to Barb describe her afternoon at the historical society. She had, indeed, seen the Raving Lunatic despite her best efforts to hide in the restroom.

"I just couldn't stay in there any longer. Someone kept shaking the handle and making little moaning sounds," she told us. "I had just come out and slipped around the corner to the periodical area when Janet Maples (AKA Raving Lunatic) grabbed my arm. I nearly leaped on top of the table. She said she'd been thinking about us and wondered what progress we had made uncovering the secrets of the house.

"I told her, vaguely, that we are moving right along, and asked if she knew where the Clarions from 1861 & 1862 were kept. She directed me to the correct shelf and went back to the desk where she was working. I flipped through more than a year's worth of issues without finding anything. I had started back through the same July, 1861, issues again when Janet stopped in front of my desk as she prepared to leave. She said it was good to see me again and turned to go. She opened the door then stopped and turned back to me. She said, 'I keep thinking I know something about your guy, Josiah Lake. Was he the one who dug up the graveyard?'

Barb shrugged, "By the time I picked my jaw up from the table and followed her outside, she had disappeared.

Chapter 16 — October 18

After my birthday guests left, Barb and I spent our time painting the kitchen and searching for more details about Josiah's treasure. In fact, we spent so much time on these tasks that I neglected training for the agility trial I had entered.

And now the feared day had arrived. Barb asked me reasonably why I would put myself through so much stress. "If you don't want to go, don't go. Nobody's holding a gun to your head."

But I felt the obligation of my promise to Belle and so woke up at the crack of dawn and drove the thirty miles to the trial site. It was cold, crisp, and dark when I left the cozy warmth of our house to go into the bleak unknown. I was dressed for an arctic adventure with field coat, sweatshirt, long-sleeved shirt, short-sleeved t-shirt, long-johns, wool socks, hat and mittens. It was 34 degrees.

As soon as I crossed the Taconic range of mountains and entered New York, the fog covered me. I drove slowly, trying to see the edge of the road, the potential tail lights ahead of me, and any shining eyes peering out from the side of the road. Two neighbors had hit or been hit by deer in the past week.

I missed the turn off the state highway onto the country road because I couldn't see it. Then I nearly missed the trial site. Sitting as it does in a valley, it looked like Brigadoon in the early morning light with wisps of fog lifting off the fields and smudging the edges of the fence and obstacles.

After several trips to the bathroom for me and a couple of walks through the field for Sojo, we calmed down enough to register, get Sojo measured for her jump height – big dogs jump higher than small ones – and pick up the course maps for the two events I had entered: standard and tunnelers.

I had run a standard course at the run-thru so the map and variety of obstacles was familiar. I'd never seen a tunnelers course but was unsurprised to see that it consisted solely of tunnels and weave poles. Sojo loved tunnels. Getting her to run through them was no problem. Getting her to enter them from the right end and in the right order was another story. Just thinking about it made me rush to the potty-house again.

The standard course was first. I walked it and thought I had a handle on the tricky part. I had to get ahead of her and call her to me to keep her from taking a jump that was in her line-of-sight as she came off the A-frame. Everything else was pretty straight-forward, and the last two obstacles, a tunnel and a jump, were standard fare. I thought I could send her through the tunnel and catch up with her as she took the last jump.

I was hot after walking the course five or six times. I shed my hat, gloves and coat as I settled in to watch the first dogs run. It was up to 50 degrees.

Our turn finally came. I handled the tricky part off the A-frame perfectly. I was feeling triumphant as we headed to the last two obstacles. I yelled, "Tunnel," and swung my left arm out as I ran toward the final jump and the finish line. Sojo ran in the wrong end of the tunnel.

My fault, I knew. I had my body turned toward the right even though I pointed to the left. Damn! I got her over the last jump and praised her for doing exactly what I told her to. She did great. I was the problem.

I fussed at myself as I led her out of the ring, fed her a jackpot of treats, and walked back to the spot I had set up my crate and chair.

Ann, the classmate who had helped me at the run-thrus, was set up next to me. "Nice run, Ruth. You handled that jump off the A-frame perfectly," she said as I crated Sojo.

"Thanks. But DAMN! If I hadn't messed up that last tunnel, we would have Q'ed."

"Yep. Too bad," she agreed. "Last week Woodie knocked the last bar after a perfect run. I pulled him out of the jump when I slowed down. It happens. Sometimes you screw up; sometimes the dog does. That's what makes the times when everything works right even more special."

I sighed. "I'd like to find that out for myself."

"You will. If it were too easy, we'd lose interest. We need the challenge to keep us addicted."

A tall, thin woman with gray-hiding blonde hair leaned out from beside Ann, "Your first trial?"

I nodded.

"My first was a disaster. Mickey ran off, took three jumps and went to visit the leash-runner before I got her to come to me. I was mortified. I'm Charlene, by the way."

"Nice to meet you. I'm Ruth." I awkwardly reached around Ann to shake Charlene's hand.

Ann patted my arm. "Ruth, if you talk to anyone here who's competed a while you'll discover that we've all had mishaps. Lots of them. Heck, Woodie pooped on the A-frame once! And I tripped over a weave support and crashed into a jump. I have messed up more ways than I can count."

"Me, too," Charlene added. "I stepped through the weave poles at the last trial. I have been doing this for years and I stepped through the weave poles! Good grief!"

"See?" Ann said. "I have a quote on my crate by Robert Browning: 'Ah, but a man's reach should exceed his grasp, Or what's a heaven for?' I think it applies to women, too."

"OK. OK! I'll settle down. But first I've got to cool down. I'll be back in a minute. I've got to get these long johns off." It was up to 60 degrees. "I thought it was supposed to be cold in the Fall in New England," I muttered to myself as I made yet another trip up the hill to the potty-house.

When I returned, calmer and cooler, Ann caught my attention. "Ruth, Charlene lives in Centerbury, not far from you. You guys ought to hook up and ride together to trials."

Charlene agreed. "It's more fun to travel together. What's the next trial you've entered, Ruth?"

I admitted that I hadn't entered anything. I didn't really know how to find out when or where the trials were. That prompted Ann and Charlene to get out their schedules and their iPhones. We picked one in two weeks that they thought I could still get into, and I filled out my entry form and sent it off with my credit card information. Ann said I should know by mid-week if I got in.

"I am surprised that there are still outdoor trials this late," I said as I pulled off my long-sleeved shirt. "Isn't it risky?"

"Oh, sure," Charlene said. "At this trial last year it snowed."

"Snow! I'm still hot and I don't have anything else I can take off. I should have brought shorts!" The sun beat down on my bare arms, face and neck. "Next time, I'll bring a suitcase with clothes suitable for ten degrees to a hundred."

Ann reached into the large tote bag next to her and pulled out a fleece jacket and a pair of shorts. Charlene grinned, "Mine are in the car."

I laughed. "My list of trial necessities keeps getting longer."

"Don't forget raincoat, boots, fingerless gloves, and sunscreen," Charlene added.

Ann and Charlene helped me study the course map for the tunnelers run. Charlene showed me how to draw lines for my course and for Sojo's. Ann showed me where I'd need to change sides. By the time I was called to walk the course, I felt fairly comfortable with it.

I walked through it several times, memorizing where I wanted to be positioned at each tricky part. The most confusing thing was that two of the tunnels were used twice during the run but with different obstacles following them. The first time through, we did tunnel-tunnel-weave and the next time was tunnel-tunnel-tunnel. But my imaginary dog and I walked the course perfectly by our final circuit.

When the real dog and I were running, it wasn't quite the same. I got lost, couldn't remember if I was going through that pair of tunnels for the first or second time. I decided it was the second and took the tunnel. I picked wrong. I finished the course, omitting five obstacles. But it was a pretty run!

This time as I left the ring, I laughed at myself. Sojo had a good time, she did everything I asked of her, and the part of the course I ran, I did well.

I arranged my face into a big smile as I headed back to my setup. I told Ann and Charlene, "I've figured it out. I just need shorter courses."

I stayed to watch them run. I wanted to see what experience could bring to the sport. Ann and Woodie ran like a psychic pair. Woodie seemed to intuit what Ann wanted without her saying a word.

Charlene was faster than Ann. Her smooth sweeps and turns looked like she was on ice skates. Her fast Aussie glided beside her.

By the time I packed up to go home, I had promised to let them know if I got into the trial I had entered and to meet up with Charlene to travel there together. Charlene said she didn't get to go to as many trials as she used to since her family situation had changed, but she would be certain to go to that one.

Sojo and I headed home after a fun day with a new friend. I had sunburned arms and nose from too much time out of the shade. It was 77 degrees.

Chapter 17 — October 25

After I got back from the trial, Barb and I painted bedrooms. Jack and Ted came by regularly to encourage, kibitz, and praise.

"I never would have thought of using that cool gray-green with the warm antique white trim. But it works!" Jack enthused.

"It looks like a decorator chose it," said Ted in what I think he intended to be praise.

They came every day, even running out to pick up supplies for us when we ran out of paint before we ran out of wall in the new sunny yellow bathroom in Barb's upstairs.

We got into the rhythm of painting in the morning and doing research in the afternoon. Historical societies for Barb; online scouring for me.

Barb got an inspiration. Maybe some of the elderly neighbors knew something about Josiah Lake. We had met many of them when they stopped by to compliment us on the improvements we'd made to our house. Barb decided we would sit on our porch and lie in wait for our chance to pounce on unwary walkers.

One elderly couple, in particular, seemed to know something about the history of our house and its builder. "Old Uncle Joe was quite a cut-up," Alvin told us. "Do you remember the story about the honey, Maud?"

Maud, dressed like an aging gypsy or bohemian, was Alvin's polar opposite. His starched shirt, tailored suit, Wall Street look was mere bland background for her bald head wrapped in an orange and purple scarf, a red off-the-shoulder peasant blouse, and a multi-colored, multi-flounced skirt. She batted her heavily made up eyes and twitched her scarlet lips, sending ripples through the hundreds of smile lines in her cheeks and jowls. "Dahling," she drawled, "of course I remember. Who could forget the Honey Pants story?" She laughed raucously.

"Right," Alvin said stiffly. "It seems that one Sunday when all the righteous were in church, Josiah and a friend decided to go looking for a honey tree in the forest. At this time, the forest was much closer to town than it is today. We believe that only about 100 acres had been cleared for the village and the farms lay primarily east and south of town. A short walk north or west would bring you to uncleared, heavy forest."

"For God's sake, Alvin, get on with it!" Maud interrupted. She gave him a look of unmistakable marital exasperation. "Sometimes you are such an old poop!"

"I was getting to it, Maud," Alvin retorted. "It's important to understand the topological context."

Maud rolled her eyes theatrically, and followed that with a heavy sigh. "Josiah was dressed in his new wide-legged pants that were all the rage in the eighteen-teens. He followed a line of bees to an old dead tree that was so packed full of honey it was streaming down the trunk and feeding a million ants. The boys filled their hats with honey, but there was still an enormous amount of honey left in the tree. So Josiah took off his pants, tied the legs closed, and filled them with honey.

"When they marched into the village just as church was letting out, Josiah in his drawers toting a pair of dripping Honey Pants, the entire town joined in the frivolity and declared it time for a picnic. Wives went home to gather up their dinners to take to the village green, men set up games of horseshoes, and children made themselves sick sucking on Josiah's pants."

Alvin huffed, "I don't think they sucked his pants, Maud."

"Of course they did!" she laughed. "I would have." Her deep-throated guffaws were infectious. Soon Barb and I were giggling with her.

After they continued their walk, we stayed on the porch enjoying the mild evening. "God, he must have been something, that Josiah Lake."

Her tone was so wistful that I took a harder look at her. "What's up? You sound sad."

"Oh, I guess I just wish I'd known him. He seems to have been such an interesting guy. One of my colleagues, Tom Williams, was like that. He could turn a routine teachers meeting into a party. I'd like to see him again."

"Well, call him. Invite him to visit. Go visit him."

"I wish I could. He died last year," she sighed. "Maybe I just need to find some fun for myself."

I nodded. "Maybe you do. Anything I can do to help?"

Barb shook her head. "No, I'm OK. I've just been thinking about Ben lately. We were married such a long time." She paused, swallowed, then continued, "He died on Halloween last year. I'm just a little melancholy."

"Melancholy is fine once in a while. It balances the normal hilarity of life."

Barb smiled, "Right."

Just then the phone rang. Barb went inside to get it. When she returned, she handed me the phone as a tear rolled down her cheek. "It's Jo. She has sad news," she said as she walked back inside.

"Hi, Jo." I said as I mentally catalogued all the potentially bad pieces of news Jo might have to share: death, devastation, disaster.

"Oh, Ruth. I just need a friendly shoulder for a little while. I lost Shep this morning."

"What happened? I didn't know he was sick." Shep was Jo's old border collie. He had been her only roommate for years. You could find them almost every night playing Frisbee on Jo's large lawn.

"You know how much traffic we have on the Road to Nowhere, as Gerry calls it. This morning I was playing Frisbee with Shep when he saw a crow land across the road. He shot out of the bushes into the road just as a delivery truck gathered speed on its way to the kennel. The driver had no chance to stop. Shep just crumpled." She stopped to sniff. "He never regained consciousness. I held him while he took his last breaths." She drew a ragged breath. "Win and Janie helped me bury him."

"Oh, God, Jo! I am so sorry" I felt my own tears gather. "Oliver and Jess will miss him, too. They were such a happy pack, running together on the Road to Nowhere."

"Belle offered to give me a puppy or a trained older dog, but I can't face it yet. In fact, I can't face going into that empty house every night when I get home. And have nobody to greet me. Or play Frisbee with me." She sniffed again. "I wondered...could you stand a visitor again? I've been thinking that maybe I will explore living there part time. Now seems like a good time to look at houses."

"Of course I can stand a visitor! Come tomorrow."

"It won't be tomorrow. But it won't be long. I'll let you know. And I have to go now. I've got to stop talking about Shep." Another sniff. "I'll call you soon."

I whistled for Sojo and hugged her to me. I was so attached to this dog I'd had for only a few months. Jo had had Shep for 13 years.

Barb came in carrying two mugs of tea. She sat beside me, handed me a mug, and squeezed my shoulder. "Poor Jo. I feel a bit foolish for my wollycobbles earlier."

"Wollycobbles?" I asked.

"My grandmother's word. It means unsteadiness. Feeling that the world is tilting under your feet."

"I know the feeling. It's good to know it has a name," I said with a grin. "Oh, and guess what? Jo's coming to visit to look for a place to live."

"Wow! When?"

"Not sure. Soon. Poor dear. She talked to me about feeling the need for change, but I know she didn't envision changing anything without Shep. Damn! Life can be so precarious." I sighed again.

"Didn't she say Shep ran after a crow?"

I nodded.

"You know crows are symbols of many things, including death. In fact, a group of crows is called a 'murder' rather than a 'flock'. And I think because they are carrion-eaters, they've been associated with war and battles. They're always around on battle-fields, cleaning up the mess. And I think there are other symbols, too. Let me check."

She picked up her phone and Googled 'crow'. "It says they are often seen as harbingers of death. And change. They are can-ny, knowing and tricksters, playful." She lay down the phone. "I think Shep was pretty lucky to have a crow lead the way into the afterlife."

Chapter 18 — November 1

I picked Jo up at the airport on Halloween afternoon. She seemed to be in good spirits, looking forward to an adventure. She said that she was free for up to a month to figure out if she wanted to live in Vermont for a while.

As we drove to Centerbury among the still colorful trees, I told her about the symbolism of the crow that Barb had found.

"Change, playful, knowing," she repeated. "Hmm, I need to think about that."

"OK. But first think about whether you want to go with me to my agility trial tomorrow. I'd planned to ride there with Charlene, but I can change that if you want to go."

"No, I'd rather stay at your place. Walk around the village. Look at available real estate for sale or rent. If you don't mind."

I realized Jo was trying to keep her mind off missing Shep. An agility trial would be too much. "Fine with me," I said. "Then I won't be more nervous than I already am."

After dark we were entertained by ghosts, goblins, and princesses arriving at our door in hopes of good candy. I had bought it, so it was good. I believed in getting what I liked. Barb wanted to get candy she didn't like so she wouldn't eat all the leftovers. I knew I'd eat the leftovers. I might as well get the good stuff. Jo said it was a philosophical dilemma that she solved by giving out dimes.

"Pah! What fun is there in that?" I scoffed with a grin.

The next morning, I got up and was ready to leave early. Charlene picked me and Sojo up, and we headed to the All Souls Agility Trial in Millers Kill, New York, a drive of about an hour. I hadn't been to this part of Washington County before and enjoyed the drive through the village, past the large gazebo and the lovely Episcopal Church.

We met up with Ann as we arrived and set up our crates, chairs, and other paraphernalia next to each other. After we registered and picked up our course maps, we settled down for a cup of coffee and a chat.

I told them about Jo's arrival at my place, and both adamantly advocated her getting a new dog. "The only cure for missing a dog is getting another one," Ann said with finality.

By then it was time to walk the dogs and get ready for the first run. I had entered Jumpers and Standard. Jumpers was first. I studied the course, I walked it, and we ran it. Sojo knocked the next to last bar. I had taken her across it at too sharp an angle. I knew it as soon as I did it, but it was too late. Damn! I praised Sojo for her great performance and tried not to beat myself up for my mistake.

I had a long wait before I ran again, so I watched others run and tried to see what they did right and wrong. Many folks had friends video their runs so they could study them afterwards. I made myself a note to add my flip camera to my agility bag before my next trial.

When my turn finally came to run, I felt pretty good about the course. I thought I had identified all the tricky areas and knew what to do about them. We ran. We ran fast. We ran clean. And we qualified! Our first 'Q'! I hugged Sojo and nearly danced as I got her back on leash. Ann and Charlene were waiting for me as I came out of the ring. Hugs for me and treats for Sojo completed our celebration.

I had convinced myself that just the experience of running was enough. But I was wrong. Getting that teal ribbon that said "Qualifying Run" was an amazing feeling. I had proved to myself that I could!

After I came down from my First Q High, I enjoyed the rest of the trial as I never had before. Now I was more than a wannabe. I was a real agility person. I called Belle to tell her.

Charlene dropped us off at home about four o'clock. We conquering heroes marched into camp expecting adulation, but nobody was home. In fact, nobody got home until nearly six, when Barb and Jo walked up the street laden with packages.

"We got steaks at the meat market, bread at the bakery, and veggies at the corner market. Shopping here is very European," Jo announced as she spread her purchases around the kitchen counter.

"Well, you could have gone to the supermarket out on the highway," I said.

"What fun would that be?" she answered with a big smile. "I love this town. It's big enough to have what I need but not so big that I feel anonymous. I think I could live here."

"Did you check out any houses?" I asked as I opened a bottle of wine. "Want some?" I added.

Jo grinned. "Yes and yes. Barb and I wandered around looking at yard signs, and I found one cute little place a couple blocks from here with a For Sale or Rent sign. I wrote down the realtor's number. I'll call tomorrow."

"Is it the one with the pretty columns on the corners?" I asked Barb.

She smiled. "Yep. The one we picked out."

"Really? You didn't tell me that," Jo said with a slight frown.

"Nope. I didn't want to influence you. It's a great house, pretty lot, fenced back. I can't wait to see inside. And did you notice its name?" Barb asked. Then without waiting for a reply, she continued, "I hadn't noticed it before either. The plaque was partially hidden by the large yew. It's the Abraham Crowe House."

My jaw dropped. "Really?"

Barb nodded, "Really."

Jo looked back and forth between us. "I guess I better call that realtor tonight."

Chapter 19 — November 2

Jo called the realtor and set up an appointment to see the Abraham Crowe house on November 3, the earliest the realtor could meet with her.

Barb decided we needed to know as much as possible about the house before Jo looked at it. She spent most of the day digging through the historical resources she'd uncovered during the search for biographical information about Josiah Lake, or as we'd come to call him, "Our Guy."

That night over dinner, she filled us in on what she'd found. "You're not going to believe this!" she announced. "Abraham Crowe was an important member of Centerbury society from the mid-1850s until a few years before he died in 1872. He was an itinerant trance lecturer who built a spiritualist temple here in Centerbury about 1855. But his biggest claim to fame was that he married the very famous Caroline or Colly Fox, a distant relative of the Fox sisters of Hydesville, NY," she finished excitedly.

"Uh, OK," I said, looking to Jo to see her reaction. She looked as blank as I felt. "Can you give us a little more? I'm lost," I told Barb.

That's all it took to launch Barb into full lecture mode. She straightened up and started to stand but thought better of it after seeing my amused cocked eyebrow. She did, however, line up her notes, clear her throat, and declaim rather loudly for a kitchen table venue.

"1848 was an important year in Western New York: two movements began that year. The first Women's Suffrage convention was held in Seneca Falls, run by Elizabeth Cady Stanton and Lucretia Mott. And it marked the first appearance of Kate and

Margaret Fox, sisters from Hydesville, who communicated with the dead and received answers through a series of knocks or table-taps. With their first demonstration of their eventually-admitted fakery, American Spiritualism was launched.

"Kate and Maggie were aged 12 and 15 when they first began communicating with a spirit they said haunted their house. They held a demonstration with their neighbors, convincing everyone including their mother that they were speaking with a man who had been murdered in the house. As interest in the girls spread, they went to live with their much older sister, Leah, in Rochester, where they were introduced to a group of radical Quakers. By 1850, they were holding séances in New York City, attracting people such as James Fennimore Cooper, Sojourner Truth, and Mary Baker Eddy.

"As their fame grew, so did the number of imitators. Within two years, hundreds of people claimed to be able to communicate with the dead as either Mediums or Trance Lecturers. Mediums generally communicated with 'those on the other side' who had messages for the living attendees of séances. Trance Lecturers generally communicated with one specific entity, their 'spiritual guide' and delivered lectures while in a trance, channeling their guide. These Spiritual Practitioners gained wide popularity, acclaim, and often great wealth.

"Although many séances included asking and answering trivial questions about where the lost key might be found or some such, more serious questions about the nature of life and death also emerged, making the séance and lecture into a type of religious service. And meeting houses into Temples.

"Most practitioners were women but there were several famous men trance lecturers. One man from Brattleboro, for example, channeled Mark Twain. Abraham Crowe was another. He claimed the ability to channel an ancient spirit called Bah-Dru. He was quite popular, traveled all over New England and made a large fortune. While on the lecture circuit, he met, courted, and married Caroline Fox, known by her nickname, 'Colly.'

"Colly Fox Crowe was nearly as famous as her distant cousins Kate and Maggie Fox. She worked with many wealthy clients who recompensed her lavishly. She was apparently quite beautiful, with raven-black hair and eyes so dark they looked like 'ebony shining from her ivory face,' or so said one admirer.

"Colly and Abraham had a house built here in Centerbury in 1854. By then there were beginning to be a few skeptics calling the Crowes out as charlatans. So they chose to build a very unostentatious dwelling and save all the elaborate adornments for the Centerbury Spiritual Society Temple, their planned center of operations. It was closer to the river and the center of the newly developed commercial district.

"Abraham took to fame like a moth to a flame and severely singed his wings on liquor and other female mediums, the younger the better. In 1869, during one of Abraham's sold-out lectures, Colly took the stage to describe Abraham's sins and to announce her decision to heed the advice of her spiritual guide to 'remove him from her life – domestic and public.' No one questioned her actions, spiritually guided as they were.

"Abraham spent the last few years of his life trying unsuccessfully to reclaim his fame and fortune. He died nearly penniless, living with one of his few remaining supporters in Eastern Vermont.

"Colly, on the other hand, thrived. She kept her reputation of honesty and thriftiness, and died peacefully at age 88 while still living in the house Our Guy built."

Barb finished with a flourish. Jo and I applauded.

Jo said, "I'll bet you were a hell of a teacher!"

Barb nodded, "I was. And that was fun. Do you have any questions?"

I asked, "Do you know who owned the house after Colly Crowe's death?"

Barb said, "It has been owned by only three others. All women. All who kept it for many years. The last was a widow who lived there 20 years after the death of her husband."

I asked, "What about the Temple? What happened to it?"

"Oh, I forgot to tell you. Abraham Crowe caught it on fire with too many candles at a poorly attended séance shortly before he died. He apparently sneaked in without Colly's permission.

Everyone escaped, but the building burned to the ground. Some said it was Colly's curse that did it."

"Colly's curse?" I asked.

"I forgot that, too. Damn! Colly said her spiritual guide placed a curse on Abraham so that all his future endeavors would fail and his vainglory turn to dust."

"Whoa! You don't want to piss off a spiritual guide, I guess."

Barb grinned at me. "Jo, what about you? Any questions?"

I glanced at Jo and noticed tears streaming down her cheeks. "What's wrong, Jo?"

Jo took a deep breath before answering, "I guess you didn't notice the names, huh? My Shep was a border COLLIE. He was led to his death when he chased after a CROW. COLLY CROWE owned the house I'm going to look at tomorrow. She had been a FOX. There's an Aesop's Fable about the Fox and the Crow. I guess she learned the moral of that story."

She looked up at me. I shrugged. Barb opened and closed her mouth a couple of times before stammering, "Wh-who learned what moral?"

Jo said deliberately, "The fable's moral: Watch out for flatterers. You know the story – a crow holding a big piece of cheese flies past a fox. The fox wants the cheese. He tells the crow, 'I bet you have a good singing voice.' The crow begins to sing, drops the cheese, and the fox eats it. I wonder what flattery Abraham used on Colly. I bet she learned not to trust him if she kicked him out."

"I never heard that fable," I said for lack of anything relevant to add to the discussion, "but I remember The Fox and the Crow comic books from when I was a kid."

"Hmm," Barb murmured as she frowned at me. She turned to Jo, "I'm impressed you made all those connections. I feel pretty unobservant for missing the fable. I was an English teacher, after all." She looked stricken as she slapped her forehead with her palm. "And, damn! I forgot to tell you the most interesting part. I am pretty sure that Our Guy built both the house and the Temple."

Jo's mouth rounded into a surprised O-shape. "I just wish we had Colly's spiritual guide to tell what all this means."

I couldn't stand it. "I think it means we need to pay very close attention to any tapping tables we encounter at that house tomorrow."

Barb and Jo left the room. Skeptics get little respect from true believers.

Chapter 20 — November 3

The long stretch of mild weather had ended. It was raw as we walked the two blocks to look at the Abraham Crowe house. The dampness of the air was exacerbated by a strong west wind that stripped the remaining leaves off the whipping branches. A wind that cut through my jacket made me resolve to include a shopping trip for warmer clothes in my week's agenda.

A Linda Cole Realty van, sporting its owner's likeness on its side, was parked in the driveway of the Crowe house. A tall bleached blonde stood beside her portrait and dipped a curtsey before approaching us with an outstretched hand. "Jo Murphy?" she asked, looking at the three of us and correctly picking Jo.

I thought I would probably like this brassy woman with a smoker's raspy voice and a wry outlook on life frequently expressed through a cocked eyebrow and a tipped head.

Jo stepped forward, reaching out her hand to grasp Linda's. "Yes, I'm Jo. These are my friends Ruth Welborne and Barbara King who live just around the corner."

"The Josiah Lake house?" Linda asked. We nodded. "You two have been busy since you bought that place. We thank you for helping strengthen the economy of Centerbury."

"I think we probably knocked at least a tenth of a point of the unemployment rate for the state," I told her. "But we have gotten very fond of our workers. In fact, Barb offered to adopt a couple of them."

Linda smiled. "Luckily, this house doesn't need that much work, Jo. It's move-in ready and was recently inspected for structural issues. I have a copy of the report for you to look at. Since the owner paid for it, I can't let you keep it, but I did get permission to show it to prospective buyers."

Jo took the proffered report and tucked it under her arm as she walked inside. "I do want to look at the report but I want to walk through the house first." She lay the report on the kitchen table and began walking through the kitchen, dining room, and living room, nodding and smiling as she did.

The first thing I noticed as we entered the living room was the trim around the windows and the fireplace mantle. It looked like ours. I nudged Barb and pointed to the pyramids enclosed in squares at each window's corner.

Barb said, "Yep. Looks like Our Guy.

Linda looked puzzled. Barb explained that she believed that Josiah Lake had built this house for Abraham and Colly Crowe in 1854.

Linda shrugged. "I don't know. I expect you could trace some of its history at the historical society and the town offices."

"I already have." Barb looked smug.

Jo interrupted the incipient Barbara King Lecture Series with a request of her own. "Tell me about the furnace. How old is it? Is it gas or oil?"

Linda opened the cellar door, ushering Jo into the dimly lit bowels of the house.

Barb nudged me to follow. "Let's look at the underpinnings. It might further support my theory."

I leaned away from Barb. "You go ahead. I'm not really into cellars. I want to look at the flow of the rooms."

Barb gave me her "look," one I knew she had used to squelch many recalcitrant high-schoolers, but I ignored it. I didn't want her to know how intimidating she could be.

I walked through the house imagining it filled with nineteenth century spiritualists. I could see Abraham holding court next to the beautifully detailed mantel that was so like ours. His back would be to the fire as he basked in the adoration of his followers.

Colly would be across the room, perhaps looking out the window with the beautifully symmetrical trim rather than watching the fawning females surrounding her husband.

I had gotten so involved in the drama I was envisioning that I didn't hear the others come up the steps and into the kitchen.

"It looks solid and clean," Barb announced. "Let's look at the inspection report."

Jo picked it up and handed it to Barb. "You go ahead. I want to go upstairs."

Barb agreed, sitting at the table and spreading the reports pages in front of her.

I watched her for a moment before taking out my phone and beginning to take photos of all the furniture. "Linda," I called, "does the owner want to sell the furnishings that are left in the house?"

"I image she would," Linda replied. "She was willing to rent the place furnished, so I don't think there was anything here she intended to keep."

Jo looked thoughtful. "Hmm, since moving here would be a very big step for me, do you think the owner would consider some sort of rent-to-own arrangement where I could rent for 6 months? The owner would apply a portion of the rent to a down-payment if I decide to buy it, or she would keep the premium on the rent if I don't."

Linda flipped through the papers she was carrying. "We didn't discuss that. But don't you want to talk about the purchase price first?"

Jo shook her head and mumbled, "Good grief, Jo." Then she straightened her back and said, "Yes, of course. I am feeling a bit off balance."

Linda patted her arm, "Just take your time. Look around, ask questions, then we can look at the financials."

I made a list of the furnishings while Barb made notes about the inspection. Jo walked from room to room, looking, touching, and sometimes calling out a question or comment.

"There's a spot on the ceiling in the smaller bedroom. Do you know if the roof has been repaired?" Jo called as she came down the stairs, reentered the kitchen, and took a seat at the table.

Barb flipped through the report. "Nothing here," she said.

Linda looked through her folder. "That part of the roof is slate. A slater made extensive repairs three years ago. I don't see anything about a current leak."

"OK," Jo said as she jotted a few notes. "Tell me about the financials." She leaned back and looked directly at Linda.

Linda pulled a page from her stack and handed it to Jo. She leaned over Jo's back and pointed to the numbers as she spoke. "This is the original asking price. Then owner dropped the price last month by this amount, so the current asking price is this amount."

"Got it," Jo said.

Linda continued, "This is the tax appraisal amount and this, last year's taxes."

Jo nodded, pursed her lips and pulled her top lip beneath her lower teeth. "And how long has it been on the market?" she finally asked.

"About 16 months." Linda backed away from Jo's chair and sat at the table next to me.

"With no offers?" I asked her. Linda frowned in my direction but shook her head. "Then it's probably priced too high," I said as I watched Linda's expression go blank.

Jo caught it too. "OK," she said. "Let me go think about it. Would you call the owner and see if she'd be amenable to looking at a rent-to-own agreement? I want to understand my options. And what rent and term is she asking for a standard lease?"

"One year term, and this monthly rent." She pointed to another figure on the sheet. "And first and last month's rent in advance plus a $1000 deposit."

"Pets?" I asked.

Linda replied, "Yes. Another $500 deposit. Do you have pets, Jo?"

Jo shook her head, "No. Not now. But I might again."

Linda gathered up the papers, leaving the price sheet with Jo. "I will call the owner and let you know what she has to say about rent-to-own. I will get back with you as soon as I can. I have your cell phone number."

When we got home, Jo nearly exploded, "God, I love that house! It is beautiful. The trim in the living room, the floors, the porch, the columns. I love them! And I bet you're right, Barb. I bet Your Guy did build it. The construction feels so solid. Makes my house in Oklahoma feel like matchsticks. I want to live in that house. At least for a while. It has a calmness about it that I didn't expect. I think Colly Crowe ended up happy in it."

I agreed. "I could almost see her living there. Colly as a young woman married to that rock star and then as an old woman, living alone, and happily self-reliant. It's got good vibes."

Barb said, "I studied the inspection report. The house is really in good condition. It has updated plumbing and electrical within the last three years. The furnace is five years old. It needs more insulation in the attic and at the sills in the cellar. You'll probably want to paint the interior. And the exterior needs paint, but there's very little rot. That's pretty standard maintenance stuff. Of course there could be a surprise, but it's in better shape than ours was."

Jo wrung her hands. "I really would like to rent the place for a few months, leave all my stuff in Oklahoma, and just see how it feels. Then, gracefully walk away from the lease or convert it to a mortgage." She sighed. "I need to find out how that works. Do I have to make the purchase price offer now? Or is that a negotiation at the end of the lease?"

"Why don't you wait until you hear from Linda before you hyperventilate?" I told her.

Barb picked up my iPad and Googled a couple of items. "Those kinds of agreements can work several ways. I think if you decide to do that, you need to get a lawyer . I'm not saying that Linda wouldn't be honest, but she is representing the seller. You need someone to represent you."

Jo looked startled, then she nodded slightly. "Thanks, Barb. I hadn't thought of that. That's a very good idea. Do you know anyone?"

Barb clicked another item on the iPad, then wrote the name and number of an attorney down for Jo. "This is the woman we used when we bought this place. Joan Daily."

I handed Jo the inventory of furnishings I had done. "You really could move right in," I told her. "It's got everything from bedspreads to an ironing board and a skillet. Dishes, pots and pans, dishcloths, and all the furniture you need, including twin beds for the guest room. If you bring clothes and a coffee pot, you're set."

Barb looked at my list, "If you want to try to come up with a value for this so you could offer to buy it if you buy the house, I have met the woman who owns the flea market on the highway. I'm sure she would do an appraisal for you for a small fee. And probably buy anything you don't want."

Jo leaned forward, holding her head in her hands. "Thanks, Barb. I'm getting a splitting headache."

"Why don't you think about something else for a while?" I said. "Do you want to read? Take a nap? Watch a movie? Eat?"

"Eating sounds good. Let me take you out to lunch somewhere. We'll talk about something totally different."

I agreed. Barb hesitated, but after a pleading look from Jo, she acquiesced. We dressed again for a polar expedition and went to our favorite diner, Momma Mary's, run by an energetic, 50ish woman named Ruby. Mary was her Momma, she told us when we first met. Her friendliness, genuine warmth, and good food made her place our destination for a meal at least once a week. The place was clean, if not fancy, and so homey it was hard to leave it once we were there.

"Hey, Ruth and Barb!" Ruby, the proprietor, said as we entered. "Who's your friend?"

"Ruby," I said, "meet Jo Murphy, my high school friend from Arkansas who found me again in Oklahoma. Jo, this is Ruby Nelson, the owner of Vermont's best diner."

"Good to meet you, honey," Ruby beamed. "Any friend of Ruth and Barb is welcome here any time. Want some coffee to start?"

We all nodded to the offer and coffee appeared in large cups before we had stripped off our coats and settled into the booth.

"So, Ruthie," Jo said as soon as we'd sipped some coffee and placed our orders. "Sally said to ask you how many tales you've written by now."

I laughed.

Barb looked puzzled. "Tales," she said. "What kind of tales?"

"Don't you remember? I've been writing down the stories that people here tell me. You know that hippie jeweler who was born on a commune? Or the plumber who was a Viet Nam vet?"

Barb said stiffly, "And what are you going to do with these 'Tales'?" She surrounded the last word with air quotes.

"You don't remember when Sally and Belle brought me Sojo, and we were talking one night about your wanting to find out about Josiah Lake? And I said I thought I'd like to write about the people I've met? Sally said I should write in verse and call them the Centerbury Tales?" I laughed again as I remembered the silliness of my answering verse.

Barb pulled her eyebrows together and took a deep breath. "And you've been writing these tales?"

I was surprised at her tone. "Um-hmm," I replied as blandly as I could.

"Why didn't you tell me?" Barb snapped.

"Uh, I don't know. I guess I thought you knew. You've seen me writing."

Barb snorted. "I thought you were jotting stuff down in your journal or something. I didn't know you were doing serious writing."

I was beginning to get irritated. "Well, why does it matter. I'm telling you now. It wasn't a big secret. I just haven't decided what, if anything, I'll do with the tales. So I've just kept writing them when someone tells me an interesting life story."

Jo interrupted. "I think that's great, Ruthie. How many have you written?"

I thought for a moment. "Six, so far."

Barb jerked her head toward me.

"How many will you write?" Jo asked quietly, trying to turn down the intensity level.

"I don't know. I was thinking maybe twelve. Like the Canterbury ones. But I still don't know if they have any purpose other than documenting for myself the move to Vermont."

Barb set down her coffee cup with a bang. "I still think it's odd you didn't discuss your writing project with me. I *am* an English teacher."

I stared at her in disbelief. I opened my mouth but Jo interrupted me. "Barb, can we change the subject? I'm sorry I brought it up. Can you tell me, based on your experience repairing your house this year, how much you think I'd have to spend repairing the Crowe house?"

Barb leaned back and closed her eyes. She said patiently, "I thought you didn't want to talk about the house."

I puffed. "Barb, for God's sake! I'm sorry I didn't show you my Tales or ask for your opinion. I've just been writing them without thinking about what to do with them. When I was ready for an edit or a critique, of course, I'd show you. Now, can we just have a nice lunch, please?"

Jo gave me a sidelong glance but said nothing.

Barb took a breath and said, "Jo, I don't think you'd have to spend more than eight or nine thousand to get the house in tiptop shape. What do you think, Ms. Chaucer?"

I rolled my eyes and puffed again. "You're probably right, Barb. That should more than cover it."

"Can't you make that rhyme?" Barb muttered.

I pretended I didn't hear.

Chapter 21 — November 4

The next morning Jo was up before 5:00 pacing. Sojo growled to alert me, then nudged my shoulder and licked my cheek before I dragged myself out of the dream I was immersed in. It's hard to leave a spiritualist convention of crows mid-lecture.

I trudged downstairs to find Jo walking slow laps around the big central fireplace, going from kitchen to dining room to living room to kitchen, over and over. I had to dodge her as she passed in front of me, unaware of my presence.

I put on a pot of coffee and forced her to sit down with me for a cup. Only then did she speak, "I haven't slept much. I think I might be possessed."

She looked possessed. Her hair was going in fourteen directions and her eyes had a strange gleam. She stared at nothing, tapping her fingers lightly on the table edge. Suddenly she turned toward me and said flatly, "Can you find me a dog quickly? I'll need a dog in that house."

"I can have a dog lined up for you in five minutes. So could you. Call Belle, and accept her offer of either a puppy or an adult." I looked at her blank face and asked, "Jo, are you all right? If this house is causing you this much worry, I think you should forget it, get on a plane, go back to Plainview, and get on with your life."

"Maybe I should. But I can't. I have to live in that house. And I have to have a dog to do it. I am absolutely convinced of that." Her eyes pled with me to understand.

"OK." I took a deep breath. "Do you want me to call Belle and have her ship a dog here? It may take a few days to arrange it."

Jo nodded. Then shook her head. "I don't know. Yes. Call her. Ask her if she has a mostly black dog. Very little white on it. Shiny black." Her voice trailed off as she slipped back to whatever vision or voice had her attention.

"I'll call her. But I think I'll wait a while. It's only 5:15."

"Hmm? Oh, sure. Then I'll call that lawyer." She drifted away again.

Sojo's insistent nudging of my thigh informed me of my next move. She needed to go out for her morning run. As I walked with her to the back porch, I felt a prickle up my neck. Something was watching me. Sojo growled and dropped into a crouch to stare out into the dark grayness of an early November morning.

I saw two small beads of reflected light, unmoving, about three feet off the ground in the center of the yard. Then they moved in a slow diagonal to the pool of yellow light spilling over the fence from the streetlamp where they disappeared. Sojo growled again. I grabbed her collar. I didn't want her to get into a tangle with what I could now see was a fox. A large red fox, sitting in the pool of light, looking at me intently.

After several moments during which I held my breath and Sojo's collar with equal intensity, the fox stood, turned away from me and disappeared into the shadows.

I eased my grip and breathed again. Sojo launched off the porch toward the outer edge of the light pool. She sniffed, ran in circles, and returned to me whining. I tried to get her to go back out in the yard, saying softly, "Go potty. Go on, girl, go potty." But she pressed against my leg and refused to move.

I felt as dazed as Jo looked when Sojo and I returned to the kitchen. I poured a cup of coffee and sat across from Jo who was still off somewhere else. My hamster-cage mind was spinning, reliving my encounter and trying to discount it as a normal occurrence when you live at the edge of a village.

We sat silently immersed in our own thoughts for another fifteen or twenty minutes before Barb wandered in from the passageway, holding an empty mug in front of her, and murmuring, "Coffee, coffee."

I pulled myself back from the vision of the fox and looked at Barb with a little trepidation. She had been very angry with me before we went to bed. Without speaking, I pointed to the carafe sitting on the table. She poured herself a cup, cocked her head toward my nearly empty cup, and filled it when I nodded.

She sat, looked from me to Jo, back to me and smiled. "Morning," she said softly.

Jo looked at her, surprised, then nodded, "Morning, Barb." She took a drink of coffee. "Do you have a number for that lawyer, Joan Somebody?"

"I gave it to you last night, remember?" She looked at me with raised eyebrows, her unspoken question clear.

I shrugged. I had no idea what was going on.

Barb said, "It's still too early to call Joan. I'll get the number for you again in a little while. In the meantime, how about some breakfast?"

Damn! I had intended to start breakfast. But after the fox encounter I forgot. I stood and started bustling bowls and spoons onto the table. Barb stopped me, "I'll do it." She studied each of us again, "You two look like you've seen a ghost."

Neither of us said anything, although I did peek at Jo to see her peeking at me. Somehow that broke the spell, and I laughed. Jo looked startled then joined me. I finally choked out, "I think I might have."

Jo giggled, "Me, too."

We laughed again as Barb said sharply, "Might have what?"

"Seen a ghost," Jo and I said at once.

As Barb got the milk and cereal and toast on the table, I told them about my early morning visitor. Jo seemed unusually worried and asked me several times if I was sure it was a fox.

After we ate, Jo said, "I have been trying to remember exactly what happened to me. I'd like to tell you, but my memory keeps shifting. I need to write it down."

"Tell us and I'll write it down," I offered.

"Of course you will," Barb sniped.

I ignored her. I got out my notebook and pen and announced that I was ready.

Jo pursed her lips, took a breath, flexed her fingers, hunched her shoulders, sipped her coffee, and finally said, "OK."

She leaned back in her chair and shut her eyes as she began her story.

"When I went to bed last night, I went right to sleep. I had thought I wouldn't be able to go to sleep for rolling around all the details about the house, but not so. What happened next must have been a dream. But it didn't feel like one. I've been stewing since I got up about whether it was real or not. You'll have to tell me what you think.

"As I lay in bed, I saw the moonlight enter my window very brightly. It was like a lamp shining in. I thought it was odd for it to get so bright so quickly, but then I thought the moon must have been behind a cloud.

"Anyway, I saw, sitting on my window sill, the silhouette of an animal. It was backlit so I couldn't see any detail of its face, just the shape and two glowing eyes. They weren't evil-looking or scary. It was as if they were reflecting light from a source above and behind me."

I gasped. That was a good description of the eyes of the fox Sojo and I had seen. Jo was so focused on telling her story that she didn't notice my reaction, but Barb did. She shot me a look known to all teachers: the straighten-up stare.

Jo continued, "I couldn't tell what kind of animal it was. I thought at first it was a cat. I'm not sure why. Maybe because it seemed so self-contained. Then it shifted slightly and I could see its snout was long and pointed. I decided it was a dog. As I think back, I'm surprised I wasn't frightened, but I wasn't even particularly surprised at having an animal appear on my window sill. It just didn't seem threatening. If anything, it seemed, I don't know, well-intentioned. Beneficent. I just watched it as it watched me.

"After some time, the animal spoke to me. I don't think it moved its mouth. I think I could have seen that from its silhouette in profile. I could easily hear its voice, soft and whispery but with a throaty harshness. Like it was hoarse and forcing the words out so they could be heard. I wasn't startled or surprised by its voice. It seemed very natural at the time.

"I've been going over and over this, trying to get the words exactly as it said them. But each time I run through them, they seem to slip away. So write this down, Ruth, please. Here's what it said:

> I was fooled by the crow
> Taken in by his songs
> By the trinkets he brought
> By the cage he built.
> I won in the end
> Unbarred the cage
> Made it my home.
> You make it yours.

"She chanted it, rhythmically, hauntingly. Then after watching me for several minutes, as she turned to leave, I saw her long brush of a tail."

I interrupted her with a gasp, "You saw my fox!" I reconsidered, "Or I saw yours."

Jo nodded slightly and continued her story in a flat, even tone. "Suddenly the fox was facing me again, the light in her eyes directed into mine. She spoke again in the same rhythmic whisper:

> Take with you Ebony
> Let night hold back night
> My kin will comfort.

And then she was gone."

Barb took a deep breath, "That was some dream!"

Jo shrugged. "I'm not sure it was a dream." She paused and looked upward before asking, "Ruth, would you read back to me what she said?"

I read it to her twice. She nodded. "It's an incantation, I think." She looked at each of us then asked, "Now do you see why I have to talk to Belle?"

I shook my head and shrugged my shoulders, "No. Sorry, Jo. I'm lost."

Barb shook her head sadly, "I don't understand either, Jo."

Jo leaned back into her chair as if exhausted. "Ebony is the name of the dog I have to get. A very black dog who will live with me in the house."

Barb asked softly, "Why do you have to get a dog?"

Jo answered as she rose from the table and moved toward the stairs, "To hold back the night."

During Jo's two-hour absence, sleeping we hoped, Barb and I tried to understand the fox's chant. Barb decided the fox was Colly Fox Crowe. "Did you notice that Jo called the fox she? It all fits, Ruth. Read that first part again."

I agreed. It fit. "Maybe Jo got up to go to the bathroom and saw the fox I saw out on the lawn. Then conflated the real fox with Colly Fox Crowe in her dream."

Barb nodded. "Yeah, that makes sense."

"But I don't know about the black dog. Border collies usually have a lot of white on them, but maybe Belle knows of a mostly black one."

I waited until 8:00 to call BellWhether Kennels. Belle answered on the first ring. I told her Jo was thinking of renting a house and staying here for a few months, she wanted a dog to share her house, and she seemed determined to have a nearly solid black border collie.

Belle said, "How could you possibly have known? I got one of my dogs back yesterday. His owner had to be put in a nursing home after a severe stroke. Nobody could keep the dog. A neighbor remembered that Mrs. Fox had gotten the dog from us, so she called to see if we could take him back. It's often hard to place dogs who have very little white on them, but Mrs. Fox fell for Evan the moment she saw him."

"What did you say his name was? And who was the owner?"

"His name is Evan. His owner is Abigail Fox, why?"

"Oh, I just want to get it straight to tell Jo." I hedged.

"I think they'd make a good match. Evan is a large male, four years old, solid as a rock. He has a sweet temperament with a spark of mischief. He actually reminds me of Jo's old dog, Shep. Same kind of presence."

I thanked Belle and told her I was sure Jo would be calling her soon. When I went back to the living room to tell Barb, Jo followed me in. I told them both what Belle had said. Barb's wide-eyed disbelief was balanced by Jo's slight smile.

Chapter 22 — November 7

I sat at my breakfast table, coffee cup in hand, staring glassy-eyed around me. I fully expected to see all my furniture up-ended, the paintings hanging askew, and holes in the roof allowing rays of sunshine to spotlight the destruction.

As I shifted my focus to the actual, I realized that all was calm. There was no devastation. The Oklahoma Tornado had gone, leaving only the wake of her turbulence behind.

I sighed and closed the cover of my journal.

Barb's fuss about my not showing her my writing made me realize how little of it I had done lately. Before I moved here, I was writing regularly. When Gerry Krane and I became Proofing Pals, she encouraged me to write about the lessons I had learned while traveling for my job and to publish them in a blog. So I did. It surprised me how well-received my stories were. Gerry was even trying to convince me to bundle up a couple dozen of them and make them into a book. She was a self-publishing expert after completing BellWhether Tails, her book about Sally and Belle.

But I hadn't written even one blog post since landing in Vermont. In fact, the short entry in my journal today was all I'd written in months other than the brief character sketches I was creating from the stories people told me.

I knew I wasn't ready to share those sketches yet. They still felt too private, like I was parading around in my underwear. Of course, I realized that I generally do have on underwear, but it's normally covered with a publicly acceptable outer layer. My sketches didn't have on their outer clothes yet.

But I hadn't even told Barb about my blog. And it was fully dressed. What was I afraid of?

Hell, I was tired of thinking. I needed to get up and do something constructive like wash dishes or sweep up dog hair. But I didn't move. I was tired. Jo had worn me out as she jumped from near catatonia to manic, frantic activity.

Within three days she had nearly everything settled. She had met with the lawyer who had drawn up an offer for the Abraham Crowe house with a rent-to-own provision and a Personal Items Purchase rider. Then she and the lawyer presented the offer to the realtor who contacted the owner, and after several counter-offers, produced an agreement that gave Jo access to the house this afternoon.

She and Barb drove to Albany where Jo was going to lease a car, go to the mall to pick up a few necessities like sheets and towels, and stop at the airport to retrieve Evan. Belle had really outdone herself getting that dog shipped out so quickly.

I was still sitting absently petting Sojo's head and wondering about how she and Evan would get along, when my doorbell rang. Normally Sojo warned me before the bell sounded, but she seemed to be as pensively lethargic as I was.

Standing at the front door wearing a big smile was Stan Cook, the contractor who had rebuilt my porch. He squatted down to Sojo's eye-level and studied her carefully. "Looks like she's settled in well. Oh, yeah."

I agreed. "I can't remember life without her. She and I are a team. Literally. We've been running agility trials over in New York, at Miller's Kill. Want some coffee?"

"Oh, yeah. Coffee'd be great. I bet you wondered what happened to me."

"I just figured you had a very slow estimation process. Four months for a bid on painting our house and fixing the rot in the mud room wall?" I raised my eyebrows. "Is that your norm?"

Stan looked sheepish. "No. I'm sorry it's taken so long. I've just had a lot going on. And now it's too late in the year to paint. But here are the estimates. I can repair the rotten wall in the mudroom for $5000. I'll do it either fixed bid or time and material. You know how my guys work. They don't mess around. You're still happy with the front porch?"

"Oh, yes. It looks beautiful. We've had lots of compliments. But what about painting?"

"To do the whole place, both sides, painting, repairing or replacing rotten wood and stuff as we find it, is going to be Twenty Grand"

I gasped.

"I know. I know it's expensive. But that includes removing, repairing, and repainting all the shutters. You've got 52 of them. Did you know that? And I'll put up new gutters and new drip edge. That'll help preserve the paint-job once it's done."

"Could you do the gutters and drip edge now? I noticed with the last rain that there was a waterfall at the side garage door. And could you prop up the mudroom wall so it doesn't collapse under the snow this winter?"

Stan thought a minute. "I could start that next week. It shouldn't take more than three or four days. Then I can do the painting first thing in the Spring. As soon as it gets warm enough."

"I need to discuss the painting with Barb, but let's go ahead with the gutters and repairing any rot that's going to cause us problems before Spring. If you'll go outside with me, I'll show you a couple of places that worry me."

We walked around the house, I pointed out my areas of concern, and Stan noted a few others. He talked as we went, telling me about himself, his kids, and other houses he'd worked on.

"I don't believe in screwing people. I've seen it too much. Guys do a crap job and leave you in a mess. I'll put up gutters in these three spots," he pointed, "fix the drip edge around the garage, fix the rotten spot at the roofline of the connector, and prop up the mudroom wall. I'll do that time and material and subtract it from the other bids. OK?" He wrote as he spoke, handing me a copy of the revised estimate when he finished.

"OK. Go ahead and do that work now. I'll let you know about the rest after I've discussed it with Barb."

Stan stuck out his hand for a firm shake. "See you Monday, Sojo."

As Stan pulled out of the driveway, Barb pulled in. He beeped his horn, and Barb waved as she walked to the door.

"Was that Stan?" she asked as soon as she got inside.

"Yep. He brought us a bid to paint the house and repair the mudroom wall." I told her the entire story as she poured a cup of coffee, played with Sojo, and settled down at the table.

"I agree with you," she said at last. "Let's do necessary now and the rest next Spring."

"Good. We'll give him the signed agreement when he comes next week." I smiled, "That's a relief. I was starting to worry about winter coming."

"Worrying won't stop it," Barb said dryly. "But I know what you mean. It will be our first winter in Vermont and I'm not too sure what to expect." She fidgeted with her coffee cup and added, "Cold and gray, I suppose."

She continued to pick up and set down her cup, shift her weight, stare at the estimate, and look very uncomfortable.

"What's up with you?" I asked her. "You're nervous as a cornered rabbit."

She gave me a half-grin. "I guess it would be nervous." She smoothed her hands across the table. "OK. I'm worrying about several things. Winter is one of them. I wonder if we will be able to keep warm. I worry about the cost of fuel. I don't know how I will do with weeks of cold and gray.

"I'm also worried about Jo. She's diving into this with very little planning. At least we had months to think and plan and worry about winter. She barely knew where Vermont was a month ago.

"And I also worry about the dog and the house she's getting. It's all so fast." She sighed and leaned back heavily in her chair.

"I know," I said. "I worry, too. But nothing she's done is irrevocable. She could send the dog back to Belle and cancel the lease agreement with thirty-days' notice. It will be OK."

Barb smiled weakly. "And I worry I've upset you. I had no right to raise such a fuss because you hadn't shown me your stories. I guess I was hurt that you didn't want me to read them."

"I understand. I'm sorry I didn't tell you about them. I guess I was afraid you'd think they were silly or unimportant or not good enough." I took a breath and said softly, "I'm just not ready to share them yet."

Shortly afterward, I heard Sojo bark then break into a long "roo-roo-roo." I was astonished to hear an echo from the back yard. I hurried to open the door as another "roo-roo-roo" call and reply sounded from kitchen and yard. I could see Jo walking a large black dog on a leash. She chuckled as her dog echoed Sojo yet again.

"Jo, he's beautiful. But BIG! And he roo-roos.

"I can't believe it. I'd never heard any dog make that sound until Sojo, and now here's another." She patted his head. "I guess that cinches it – he belongs here with us."

Sojo was pushing against my legs to get out the door. I opened it wider and she darted out then stopped short when she saw Evan. She slowly walked to him, sniffing the air around him, and doing a twisty dance as she got in close.

Evan responded to her with sniff-for-sniff and twist-for-twist attention. When they were within touching distance, Evan licked her ear while Sojo leaned against him.

"What the hell?" Jo exclaimed. "These guys act like it's a re-union instead of an introduction. Could they know each other?" she asked as she unclipped Evan from the leash. He took off, running the length of the yard with Sojo by his side. They ran and ran. Finally Sojo came up the stairs and dashed in beside me headed to her water dish. Evan followed and waited patiently until she finished before lapping up the remainder of the water and whining at me.

"Do you want more?" I refilled the bowl and set it beside him. He drank again, leaving only a little for Sojo to finish.

Barb watched in astonishment. "I guess I can quit worrying about Evan fitting in."

Both dogs collapsed on the floor, lying close to each other. From that angle, it was clear they looked very alike if you ignored their coloring. Both had ears that tipped forward and a sloping rather than a vertical stop between the nose and the forehead. Neither had the blocky head of the recent Australian imports.

After comparing them again, I asked Jo, "Did Belle send you Evan's pedigree?" as I retrieved Sojo's from the file drawer in the hallway.

She pulled an envelope from her purse and handed it to me. I took out the pedigree and spread it on the counter next to Sojo's. "I'll be damned!" I said moments later.

Barb and Jo huddled around me to see for themselves what was clearly spelled out in black and white: Sojo and Evan had exactly the same pedigrees. They were brother and sister. Littermates."

"I wonder why Belle didn't tell me," Jo muttered.

Barb raised an eyebrow. "Would it have made any difference?"

"No," Jo admitted. "I knew he was mine the second I heard his name."

Chapter 23 — November 9

Jo and Evan moved into the Abraham Crowe house as planned. Barb and I helped her make up the beds, find all the light switches, and get the boiler up to temperature.

After dinner at my place, Jo and Evan marched out into the cold for their first night in their new home. Jo was excited about the adventure. Barb and I reassured ourselves by stating the obvious again and again: "She's just around the corner." "She'll be alright." "We can be there in five minutes." "She has Evan." It finally sorted down to Evan – he would somehow make everything fine.

The next morning, I woke up early, eager to hear from Jo about her first night. She didn't call until nearly ten o'clock. When I saw her name on my cell phone, I answered with an abrupt "Are you OK? I've been worried."

Jo laughed. "Believe it or not, I just woke up. I crawled into that old bed last night, Evan curled up beside me, and I crashed. I haven't slept much lately. I guess I made up for lost time. I'm going to take Evan out for a walk in a little while. We'll stop by if you'll be home."

About forty-five minutes later, they arrived. It was a cool, crisp morning. Jo's cheeks were rosy from her brisk walk in the morning air. Evan was delighted to see Sojo. They adjourned to the backyard for a thorough romp. They had already established a pattern to their play – Sojo would flatten down next to the big sugar maple, waiting to pounce on Evan as he flew past. Then together they would circumnavigate the property before starting the loop again.

Jo, Barb, and I sat on the back porch I had recently enclosed with glass storm windows, replacing the screens of summer. It was a perfect place to sit in the late morning and enjoy our dogs. Unfortunately, it didn't last long. The phone and the doorbell rang simultaneously. I went for the phone while Barb answered the door.

"This is Janet Maples," I heard with dawning dread. "I understand you have been asking for me."

"Oh, hello, Janet. This is Ruth. I think Barb was trying to reach you. Let me get her for you." I held the phone at arm's length as if it were a wriggling copperhead and went in search of Barb. She was at the front door, laughing with Stan and his main man, Petey. I stuck the phone in Barb's hand whispering, "Raving Lunatic," and turned to Stan and Petey.

"Hi, guys. Ready to patch us up today?"

Stan sang out his characteristic, "Oh, yeah!" as Petey shyly mumbled, "Hey, Ruth."

I liked Petey. He was good at everything, quietly working away while his coworkers yammered about everything from baseball games to weekends at the Cape to the price of gasoline.

"Petey and Brent will get those gutters up, fix the rot and stuff." Stan said as he turned to leave.

"Thanks, Stan. Petey, you got it all lined out?"

"Yes, m'am."

"I'm around back. Yell if you have questions. The dogs are out so be sure to keep the gate closed."

"Did you get another dog, Ruth?"

"No, my friend Jo is here with her boy, Evan. He and Sojo are pals already."

"I'll stop by and play with them. See you later," he said, loping toward his truck.

I was so happy Petey was working here that I nearly forgot about Janet Maples' phone call until I saw the stricken expression on Barb's face.

"What's up?" I asked.

"I really screwed up," Jo confessed.

"No," Barb said, "you couldn't have known."

"Known what?" I demanded.

"I was talking to Janet and trying gracefully to get rid of her. Jo overheard me and thought I was putting Janet off because of Jo's being here. So Jo said, rather loudly, that I should invite Janet over to see Jo's new house. And Janet heard. And accepted. She will meet us at three o'clock."

"Oh, no!" I moaned. "What have you done?" I threw my arms into the air in mock despair.

Jo said quietly, "Oh, she can't be that bad."

Barb and I only looked at her.

"OK, she can be that bad, but I'll deal with her. You can just sit back and observe."

Barb and I burst out laughing.

As we got ready to go to Jo's that afternoon, Petey knocked on my door. "Hey, Ruth. Could you come out here for a minute? I want to show you something."

"Sure. Let me get Barb. She'll want to see, too." I waited for Barb, and we both followed Petey to the front of the house where he had pulled off part of the roof at the front of the connector room.

I climbed the ladder as he indicated and looked into the hole. "Look over at the wall to Barb's house," Petey said. There, attached to the wall, was a small wooden box, wrapped with iron bands. It was held in place by a rusty iron bracket that fit over the handle on top of the box.

"Wow!" I said as I climbed down.

Barb nearly knocked me over so she could get to the top. After looking at the box and trying to remove it, she scrambled back down. "I'll bet it's the next clue! Can you get it down, Petey?"

"Yes, m'am. But I don't have the right tools today. I'll get it down in the morning." He carried the ladder back to his truck. "See you tomorrow!" he called as he drove away.

Barb's mind was churning. I could see it in her jittery weight-shifting from foot to foot. "I can't stand it! We have to wait 'til tomorrow to see what's in Josiah's box. What a strange place to put it. Why do you think he put it there? Of course, all his boxes have been in strange places. I mean, in the oven for heaven's sake."

"Barb, chill," I directed. "We have to wait. And right now we have to go."

Ten minutes later we walked into Jo's new quarters. They already seemed cozier, just from her and Evan's presence. Luckily we arrived before the Raving Lunatic. We had time to tell Jo about our latest find.

"And DO NOT mention it to Janet Maples," Barb warned sternly.

"Oh, I won't. I know better than that."

Barb looked hard at Jo.

"OK. I know better than that, now." Jo admitted.

Just then the bell rang. I took a deep breath. Barb leaned back and closed her eyes. Jo went to answer the door.

Janet looked even more wren-ish than the last time I saw her: she wore a shaggy cardigan in a mixture of dull browns and grays; her braid had come loose letting wisps of hair feather out in all directions. I introduced Jo to her as an old friend of mine and the new tenant of the Abraham Crowe house.

Janet graciously welcomed her to Vermont then said with some asperity, "It rankles me that this is called the Abraham Crowe house. He may have been here when it was built, but it was always Colly's. She lived here many years. Died here. It should be named the Colly Crowe house!"

I caught Barb's look of astonishment and knew it must mirror my own. That was the most sensible statement I had ever heard Janet Maples utter.

"I get so exercised about the invisibility of women," she continued. "As an historian, it is particularly galling to find so few clues about the contribution of women to the overall collective knowledge-base of the species from a Western perspective. Unless it is directly related to women's health or childbirth. And even then, men tend to belittle any anecdotal wisdom that women put forward." She finally stopped for a breath before launching again. "Of course, many of the quote primitive societies end-quote recognize the Great Maternal and honor her. My own heritage, for example, has a strong matrilineal tradition." She pulled herself up to her full five-foot height and said sadly, "But I cannot right every wrong. I can only interpret the sacred as I see it."

Damn! She derailed just as I thought she was making sense. I glanced at Barb. She widened her eyes in mock-surprise. I had to cough to cover a chuckle that tried desperately to escape.

Jo asked Janet if she would like to see the house, but Janet was already engrossed in the window frame. She turned her attention to Jo only to request a ruler. Jo produced a yardstick from some closet's corner as Janet pulled out pen and paper and began to mutter, "The three levels of the molding, the triad, the three faces of the moon, three Fates, three Graces, three Sirens, three witches, three Furies. Women in threes." She stopped suddenly and darted glances at each of us. "Women in threes," she said again. "Oh, my!" She dropped her pen and closed her eyes.

The three of us barely moved. I know I was holding my breath. Jo simply looked stunned. After a moment, Janet leaned forward and said softly, "So it begins." Then standing suddenly she took the yardstick from Jo's still outstretched hand. "Thank you, dear. Let me just jot down these measurements."

The remainder of Janet's visit continued in the same vein: she would jump from discussing a feature of the house to a dizzying list of related symbols without taking a breath; then she would rein herself in for a minute or two before falling down the rabbit hole again. It was exhausting. When she finally left, the three of us sat in silence, spellbound. Literally. Bound by her spell. Evan's whining from the back porch finally pulled us back to the surface.

The next morning, Petey arrived with his full set of tools and quickly removed the box from its hiding place. As he handed it down the ladder to me, I felt the hairs on the back of my neck prickle. Choosing to ignore my unease, I hurried to the porch where Barb was waiting with a tarp spread across the floor. "Why the tarp?" I asked as I put the box on the table.

"I don't want to lose anything through the cracks," she replied.

I thought that would be a good motto. Janet Maples should heed it. I started to tell Barb my observation when she gave a little cry. She had opened the box.

She looked inside then muttered an uncharacteristic "Damn! Damn! Damn!" She picked the box up, held it upside down, shook it, and slammed it back on the table. "Damn!"

I peered into the box. I didn't see anything either, but I thought a closer examination might be necessary. I found my flashlight and shined it into the box. Was something caught in the corners? Was it papered with newsprint? No to both. Then I noticed there was some sort of lettering around the bottom walls of the box. Impossible to read. I couldn't get the light or my trifocals into any configuration that let me see the lettering.

Barb lost patience with my contortions and grabbed both the box and the flashlight. "Let's take this damned thing apart," she demanded.

"Set it down a minute, Barb. I think we can get those bands off. See here?" I pointed to what looked like a joint in the metal. We took turns pulling and twisting the bands until Barb discovered they fit together like a Greek key. When she slid one side up and the other over and down, the band fell off in her hand. The other side worked in reverse.

I was fascinated by the intricacy of the construction. I played with the pieces, trying to put them back together. Barb grabbed them away from me and separated the five pieces of the box. After she removed the bottom, she slipped the finger joints of the four sides apart. Then she placed the sides next to each other so that the letters at the bottom of each made a single line of text:

IF YOU FOUND THIS YOU CAN FIND MORE.

Chapter 24 — November 11

Armistice Day. Red poppies of Flanders. I remember old women selling little wire-stemmed boutonnieres in front of departments stores in the Fifties. My grandma always bought us each one, in remembrance of her brother who was in the Great War.

I didn't know what about war was Great nor why she wanted to remember her brother. I wanted to forget mine. But I always wore a poppy for Grandma's brother. I'd wear one today if I could find one.

I lay down my journal and turned on the television. I had been so preoccupied with Jo, the Raving Lunatic, crows, foxes and empty boxes that I realized I had no idea of what was happening in the world. The news channels buzzed with current and impending disasters: wars (Great or not) in Central Africa, Ukraine, Syria, Iraq, Chicago, Gaza, and a small town in Missouri.

I felt battered and depressed after fifteen minutes of watching but was too hypnotized by the shrieking crawl line to move. Luckily, Sojo came to my rescue with her orange ball and a "roo-roo-roo."

"You're right, Soj," I told her. "It's too nice outside to sit in here."

I threw the ball from the top of the porch. She ran after it, but stopped before retrieving it and barked at something at the end of the house. She continued to bark even after I called her to me. I went to investigate. As I neared the back corner, I could hear a radio softly playing an old tune by the Supremes and someone singing along, missing some of the words but hitting the "Stop in the Name of Love" chorus with gusto.

I peeped around the corner and saw a man with a paint can and paint brush busily whitening a newly installed clapboard. "Hello," I said loudly. He leaped backward, startled. "Sorry," I chuckled, "I didn't mean to frighten you. I'm Ruth Welborne. This is my house."

"Pleased to meet youse. I'm Gary. Stan told me to go ahead and paint these replacement boards since it's warm enough for paint to dry."

We chatted for a few minutes until Sojo threw her ball at my feet. "I guess that's a hint that someone is impatient. I'd better go. She won't give up."

Gary grinned, "That's a border collie for youse."

I walked away wonder where he was from. New Jersey? His was not an accent I'd heard in Vermont.

Petey joined me in the back yard, stopping to throw the ball for Sojo. "I've got to go get a couple things before we can finish here. Did you meet Gary?" When I nodded, he continued, "He's Stan's brother-in-law."

"Ah," I said knowingly although I had no clue what that signified. Did family trump seniority in Stan's pantheon? I didn't ask. I didn't want to hear about any internecine wars in the contractor's crew today.

The unseasonably warm November sun felt good on my face as I sat on my little deck. I liked this spot. It was tucked between the house and the garage on the back side of the breezeway and best of all, it was invisible except from inside the breezeway or from the driveway within a few feet of the back fence. I often sat there after playing with Sojo. She was lying at my feet, sounding tiny yips as she slept. Her eyes rolled, her legs periodically flexed, and the tip of her tail twitched. I wondered if there was a canine Freudian interpretation of dog dreams. One that tied their lip movements to their litter days of fighting for a teat? More thoughts flickered across my field of awareness – ideas for new ways to handle tight turns at the agility trial, a list of items to pick up from the grocery story, and something about a wool skirt hanging in my closet – when my head fell forward and bounced my chin on my chest.

I dangled my hand off the arm of my chair, unwilling to move yet. Sojo nudged her head under my palm at the same moment a loud blast of guitar music, I think from "Louie, Lou-ie," startled us both. A sheepish Gary poked his head around the corner of the house saying, "Sorry! I knocked the radio off the ladder and hit the volume button when I tried to catch it."

"'Sawright," I mumbled. I fluttered my fingers at him and settled back into my chair. I thought I just might catch another snooze, but my nap was doomed. Barb's mudroom door slammed, and a few seconds later, she entered my field of vision. I decided to keep quiet and watch. I really didn't want to get sucked into helping her with another project.

She had what looked like a camera around her neck and carried a step ladder. She backed out into the yard about twenty feet and set up the ladder. She climbed up a couple of steps, held the camera in front of her and pointed it at the end of her mudroom. She slowly panned the length of her house and the length of mine. She aimed low at the foundation and moved the camera horizontally to the roof before turning slightly to the right and starting again.

As she finally turned the camera in my direction, I waved and said loudly, "What are you doing?"

She nearly fell off the ladder. "I didn't know you were there." She climbed down and walked toward me, patting Sojo along the way. Sojo adored Barb. The two of them joined me on the deck. Barb took the camera off her neck and fiddled with the dials on the back. "Hmm," she said as she scooted her chair into the shade. "Just a sec." She pushed buttons, frowning, and said, "That doesn't look right."

"What are you doing?" I asked again.

She continued to flick buttons and frown. "I need to reshoot some of this," she said, turning back to the ladder without answering me.

She spent nearly an hour repositioning her ladder, encircling the house, panning areas, reviewing the digital output, and retaking various angles. I had tired of watching and was in my living room reading when she marched through the door purposefully and shoved the camera under my nose. "Look at that!" she commanded.

I looked but could make out nothing. I pushed the camera out a few inches. "Trifocals," I said. I looked again. And still saw only white, yellow, orange, magenta, and indigo shapes. "What am I looking at?" I asked.

"God, Ruth! It's your breezeway!"

I still saw nothing recognizable. "OK," I muttered. I tried turning the camera a quarter-turn. Maybe I needed to look at it in portrait mode.

Barb grabbed the camera, turned it back to the horizontal, and stabbed a finger at a dark blue square on the screen. "That is a void!" She sat down with a huff. "Oh, sorry. I'm just frustrated because I can't make this damned thing work."

"What are you doing?" I asked for the third time.

"Taking pictures of ghosts," she snapped.

"Is this a ghost-buster camera? A Spectermatic? A Ghouleroid?"

"No, smartass, it is an infrared or thermal camera. I'm trying to see inside the walls."

"Where did you get it? Aren't they expensive?"

"Rented it online. I'm trying to see empty space, hidden compartments. Something like that." She pointed again at a dark blue area of the image.

"What is it?"

"Nothing."

"Nothing?"

"Right. Nothing where something should be. An empty space between your breezeway and the garage."

I frowned. "There's a closet there."

"Above the closet."

"My office is above the closet."

"Between your office and the closet."

"The floor of my office. The ceiling of the closet. Barb, have you been drinking?"

"No, I have not been drinking, but I think there is an anomaly under your office floor. I think it's worth exploring." She was getting irritated.

I looked at the image again. I still saw nothing that made sense, but I do know how floors are constructed. I said patiently, "There are floor joists about every sixteen inches. Between them is nothing. That's what is supposed to be there."

"Then what is that?" Barb pointed at a dark rectangle.

"Beats me."

"You don't think it's odd to find a box shape between your floor joists?"

"God, I don't know, Barb. What's your point?" My patience was evaporating by the minute.

"I think there's something hidden there." She snapped.

"There might be. But if so, it was put there after 1974 when the garage and office were built."

"Oh! I forgot about that." She deflated onto the couch. "I still think there's something there."

"Well, OK, then. Let's look."

"We may have to tear up the floor."

"In that case, let me see if Petey's still outside."

Petey made quick work of pulling up the edges of the carpet, locating the patched plywood, and lifting the "hatch," as he called it, off the joists. Underneath was an old wooden cigar box, its paper label pealing and all but illegible, lying on the sheetrock of the ceiling below. Petey retrieved it, handed it to Barb, and re-assembled the floor.

Barb, meanwhile, opened the box. It was filled with pieces of paper, all torn to be about four inches by six inches. Most had childish writing on them. Some looked like arithmetic problems and others like spelling words. "Homework," Barb muttered. "Some kid saved her homework." She leaned against the wall in resignation. "Dammit, Ruth. I thought I had found something."

I shuffled through the sheets of paper until I found a little hand-made booklet. There were about fifteen pages held together by a string that was tied though holes punched in the upper left corner of each page.

The first page, written in red pencil, said *"TRESHUR GUYD"*.

Barb said, "Under ten. Eight for a girl."

"OK," I shrugged. I didn't know what she meant, but I really didn't care.

She started to explain why she thought the age of the writer was as she had announced until I hushed her with a question, "OK. OK. What else does the booklet say?"

She lay the booklet on the floor between us and turned the page:

> CLUS
> Newspaper articals
> Cigret boxs
> Gold
> Letter

The next page was similar in format:

> LOCASHUNS
> Basemunt fireplace
> Ovin
> Basemunt seeling
> Little fireplace room
> Roof of hall
> Under old porch

The rest of the booklet was blank.

We examined all the other sheets in the box, but none were more than they seemed: pieces of homework worksheets printed in purple mimeograph ink.

"Wow," I said. "I haven't seen mimeographs in years."

Barb shut me down quickly, "This is just junk. It's the booklet that matters. Don't you see? Whoever wrote this had found Josiah's clues. Only they found one more than we have. Under the old porch."

"Which one is the Old Porch?" I asked rationally. We had five porches between us.

"I'll just have to use my camera on all of them." She bounced down the stairs and out into the backyard, eager to use her magic camera again. But after two hours of searching, she had found nothing. She even constructed a reverse periscope with a hoe handle, a mirror, and a piece of flexible tube. No luck.

By evening, Barb was out of sorts and spoiling for an argument. I tried to stay out of her way. After all, this was Armistice Day. I didn't need to start a war of my own.

Chapter 25 — November 26

We have to be invested in rituals for them to comfort us. I asked each of my guests to bring something for dinner that was part of their family's ritual: cranberry relish, pumpkin pie, sweet potato casserole, whatever made them feel like home. We combined everyone's offerings with my turkey and dressing to create a feast that satisfied the eye, mouth, and spirit. And for that we gave thanks.

I sent home plates of food with Jo and The Boys – Jack and Ted – but both Barb's and my refrigerators were still stuffed with leftovers. I stood in front of that appliance's door, trying to conjure up something for breakfast. I could hear Barb on the phone in her kitchen. She sounded excited – her words came quickly and her voice was pitched higher than its normal mezzo range.

Within a few minutes, she hurried through the door of the passageway to share her news. "Guess what, Ruth, I just got a call from Sherry Pine. She grew up in this house. Her parents bought it in the early Seventies, and her mother lived here until she died last year. We bought it from the Pine Trust, remember?"

I nodded.

She continued, "You know I'd been trying to reach one of the Pine children to ask about the *TRESHUR GUYD*. The realtor's office finally reached Sherry, who called me. Unfortunately, Sherry doesn't know anything about the box. She said she was just the baby in the family and got left out of most games. Sounds a little bitter. Anyway, she thinks one of her older sisters probably hid the box. She said they were always hiding things from her, and burying time capsules in the yard. But she did promise to ask them to contact me."

"Hmm. That's nice. Want some fried stuffing and eggs for breakfast?"

"Good heavens, no. Are you really going to eat that?"

"Yep. It'll be great. Like hash and eggs."

She wrinkled her nose, "Go for it. I'll eat cold pie." She looked in the refrigerator. "Where is it?"

"Split up and sent home with Jo and The Boys. Sure you don't want some stuffing and eggs. I pulled a skillet out and placed it on a burner. Maybe I would actually fix it. I had mainly been razzing Barb, but why not? It had sausage and bread in it. Sounded like breakfast to me.

Barb grudgingly tasted a bite after I had browned it and cooked a couple eggs on top of it. She even went back for seconds. We decided to make a new ritual of stuffing and eggs for the morning after.

That afternoon while I was out playing ball with Sojo, Ted called me to the back fence. He was escorting his horse-sized Labrador retriever puppy across the field behind our yard. "I want to thank you again for having us to dinner yesterday. It was great! And we are so happy you two moved to the neighborhood. Are you still glad you made the move?"

"So far," I smiled.

"Right. You haven't been through a winter yet. Oh, honey! But you'll be OK. Just remember not to hibernate. Get out whenever you can. Stay active. It makes the long cold nights pass faster. Our first winter here, we made the mistake of staying in if there was a flake of snow in the air or on the ground. Remember, we moved here from the desert. Honey, snow wasn't a word in our vocabulary. But staying inside all winter made us pale – pale of skin and pale of spirit. I even bought a sunlamp. I'm sure I have SAD. I grew up in the sun. I always had a great tan. And a body worth showing off, then. I got lots of attention. Oh, the ravages of time!"

"Anyway," he continued, "we learned to go outside for a while every time the sun shines, even if it's ball-shrinking cold. Just get some sun on your face.

"And escape for a week or two. Go somewhere sunny – Mexico, Florida, the Caribbean, Arizona. It doesn't matter where. Just get sun. We like to go in late January or early February. I think this year we'll go to Arizona to check on our property, then to Baja for a few days. Those boys in Speedos help raise my, um, spirits, too.

I laughed, "You really are bad!" I raised an eyebrow. "Thanks for the advice. I'll give it some thought. Even about the boys in Speedos." I waved my fingers over my shoulder as I turned back to my impatiently waiting dog. She was standing in the classic border collie crouch looking pointedly at the ball, at me, at the ball, at me. "OK," I agreed. "Bring it here."

"Roo-roo-roo," she sang happily as she chased after her ball.

Jo called to me from Barb's kitchen, "Come have some coffee with us."

I complied. "I've been meaning to ask you how you're feeling about your house by now."

Jo's expression softened. "Once I got over expecting to see spectral foxes around every corner, I love it out of all proportion. It has a feeling of home that I never had in Plainview. Speaking of which, I was just telling Barb that I think I'll go to Plainview for Christmas. I want to check on my house, my diner, my sister. And I'd like to bring my car and some of my things back with me."

"Hmm." I couldn't think what to say. I hadn't thought about Christmas. After talking with Ted I was caught up in imagining a February beach vacation.

Barb asked sensibly, "What about Evan?"

"I want to take him. Belle shipped him here. I guess I can ship him back," Jo answered. "Can you ship dogs in the freezing cold?"

"I'm getting an idea," I interrupted. "Barb, would you like to go to Plainview for Christmas? We could all drive there, with the dogs, then Jo could bring her own car back."

Barb's eyes widened in surprise. "I hadn't thought about it. I just assumed we would all be here. I don't know. Let me think about it."

"Ruth, are you sure you want to do that? It's a long drive." Jo was trying hard to keep the hope out of her voice.

"I know it's long. And I hadn't thought about it either. But I just got a flash of being with Jake for the holidays. I think I'd like to go."

Barb looked from one to the other of us. "You two should go. I will stay here and tend the houses."

"No," I said quickly

No," Joe echoed.

"I will not leave you here alone at Christmas," I said firmly.

"I can go visit my cousin over in New York," Barb countered.

"No. You come with us or I don't go." I said.

"That's not fair, Ruth. You're putting the whole decision on me."

I shrugged. "I'm OK with not going. I just thought it would be fun to take a road-trip, show you Plainview, introduce you to my other friends, play with Jake, and help Jo out all at the same time. But if you really don't want to go, that's fine."

Barb cocked her head and puckered her lips. "Could we stop in St. Louis on the way? I could show you how I spent the last forty years."

"It grows on you, doesn't it?" I grinned.

"We'd need to arrange for a house tender. And get the car serviced. Which car should we take? Mine is newer but yours is bigger. And stop the mail and the newspaper. Oh, I'd better get a pad and pencil. I need a list."

Jo examined Barb closely. "Are you sure? I can just fly there and ship Evan. That's what I'd planned to do."

Barb looked up from her writing, "How long will we be gone? Two weeks?"

"At least." I replied. "It will take six days just to drive there and back. If we stop in St. Louis, that will add a day. So there's a week."

Barb pulled out a calendar. "If we want to be there for Christmas, we need to leave on the 21st at the latest."

Jo added, "The 20th. I'd like to be there for Christmas Eve."

"OK," Barb made notes. "Then we could stay until the 30th and be home on the 1st."

"Unless it blizzards," I said. "We'd better add a few days of contingency on each end."

"Three days on each end. That gets us out to three weeks," Barb calculated.

"Is that a problem?" Jo asked. "I can just fly."

Barb ignored her. "Let's check with Ted and Jack. If they're here, I'll bet they'd keep an eye on our houses."

"I'll get the car serviced next week. Let's plan to be ready to leave on the 17th if the weather looks chancy."

"Right," Barb nodded.

"I can just fly," Jo said. Barb and I stared at her. "Right," she conceded.

Chapter 26 — December 3

A week of frantic activity had followed our decision to go to Oklahoma. I kept having visions of Chevy Chase and *Christmas Vacation*, but Barb and Jo assured me that we would be fine. We had planned for everything.

Jo had taken on the dogs' requirements. She spoke with the vet about car sickness and diarrhea – just in case – and had remedies on hand for each. She had a list of dog-friendly motels on our route. She had bought a canister for dog food, gallon jugs of water, and folding travel crates that would make moving in and out of motels easier. She allocated blankets to stuff around the backside of the dogs' crates in the car and to cover the crates inside the car if we got stranded.

As she ticked off her accomplishments to us, Barb moaned, "Oh, I forgot about blizzard emergency kits. We'll need blankets, food, and water. And boots! Ruth, can you check into the cost of renting a bin to strap on top of the car? That's the only way I can see we'll be able to get everything in."

I winked at Jo. "We're just going to strap the dog crates on top. Then the whole storage area and half the back seat will be empty."

"You will do no such thing, Ruth Welborne. Your name is not Mitt Romney, and I will not ride in a car with a dog strapped on top!"

Jo hooted in glee. "Barb, can I pull the other leg?"

"Very funny." She huffed twice then said with a spritz of acid, "So, Ms. Smartass, what have you done lately?"

"I got the car serviced, replaced two tires, and reconnected the 'On Star' service. I got together a small toolkit and included a

flashlight and flares. Jo, did I ever tell you about my college boyfriend who brought me a box of flares instead of a bouquet of
flowers for the Homecoming dance? I thought he might have
some odd neurological disease, but he intended to give me flares.
He said they were to keep me safe if the car broke down at night.
Sweet boy! I wonder whatever happened to Charlie." I smiled as
I remembered the looks I'd gotten when I carried a box of flares
into my dorm while wearing a pretty damned stunning evening
gown. "Barb, you remember Charlie Pearson, don't you? Tall,
thin, dark hair and eyes, a little beard?"

Barb rolled her eyes. "Yes, I remember Charlie and the
flares. Now what else have you accomplished?"

"Well, I did my laundry, I dusted the living room, and I
trimmed Sojo's toenails."

Barb gave me *the look*. She also sighed. A sure sign I was getting to her. "Did you talk to Ted and Jack?"

"Not yet. Planned for fifteen-hundred, Captain," I said with
a salute.

"Didn't you get an advanced degree in exasperating behav-
iors? What was that, again? Not an M-A. Oh, I remember, an A-
S-S."

"OK, you two. Enough. If just planning this trip gets you
into this state, I will just fly."

"No, you won't," Barb and I said in unison.

"Well, at least you agree about something!" Jo said with a
grin. "Do you two go on like that all the time?"

Barb threw an arm around my shoulder. "No, not all the
time. When she does what I tell her to, we get along fine."

I only shrugged.

I kept my promise to visit Ted and Jack. I had been in-
structed to ask them for recommendations for a house watcher.
Our expectation was that they would volunteer.

Jack had gone out, looking at fresh meat at the butcher
shop, Ted said. His constant stream of suggestive remarks, while
entertaining, could become tiresome. Jack usually served as the
brake, stopping Ted before he crossed the line.

In Jack's absence, I was prepared for an onslaught of one-liners. But he surprised me with a serious comment about watching the house while we were gone.

"Go to the hardware store and buy a thermostat-controlled plug-in. I think they're called 'Freeze Guards.' Ask one of the cute young things there if you can't find it. You plug it into an electrical socket, plug a lamp into its output socket, put a red bulb in the lamp, put the lamp in a window, and set the temperature for about fifty degrees. If the temperature drops below your set-point, the red bulb will light up, and we'll be able to see it as we walk or drive by your house. If the light is on, we'll notify you and call someone to fix the problem, or just turn tricks in your house."

"Thanks, I've never heard of such a thing."

"You've never heard of turning tricks? Where did you say you were from?" Ted asked innocently.

"Ha-ha! Freeze Guard, did you say?"

"They're about thirty dollars each, but worth it." Ted replied.

"Only thirty dollars? God, you're cheap!" I winked as he laughed.

"Oh, honey. Thirty dollars wouldn't get you in the door, even in Arizona!"

I smiled, "Did you grow up in Arizona?"

"I was born there. Stayed there until I was almost thirty. But I didn't grow up until I left." His rueful smile accompanied me out the door.

Before going home, I stopped in at Messers, the local hardware store. One of the "cute young things" in jeans and a flannel shirt asked if he could help. Trading quips with Ted had me prepped with a smart-ass reply, but the earnest helpfulness of the young man choked off my reply. "Um, ah, Freeze Guards? For alerting you if the heat goes off? With a light." I couldn't seem to construct a cogent sentence.

He studied me for a moment. I'm sure he was looking for signs of dementia or prolonged drug abuse. "Come this way," he said at last. "I think this is what you mean." He held out a package clearly marked in big red letters 'Freeze Alert'."

"That's it," I agreed. "Three. And light bulbs. Red. Three." I babbled.

He looked me over again as he picked up two more Freeze Alerts and led the way around the corner to an overwhelming display of light bulbs of all shapes, sizes, colors, wattages, and prices. "I assume you are going to use these just for the Freeze Alert?" he asked.

"Yes. I don't want them above the door. Too obvious," I said and nearly choked. I'd probably shocked the poor boy to death.

But he sputtered with laughter. "OK, then," he said. "The cheap ones will do for occasional use."

"No use at all, I hope," I said with a smile. "Thanks for the help."

When I got home, I described my meeting with Ted and the trip to Messers to Barb. She just shook her head and sighed as she added "Set Up Freeze Alerts" to the bottom of her list and checked off "Ted and Jack."

"What's left on the list?" I asked.

"Clean out fridge. Get cash. Wrap packages. Find boots. Dry run pack car."

"What do you mean 'dry run pack car'?"

"I'm worried that with only half the backseat available, we won't have room for everything. I thought if we all brought the bags and boxes we want to take – they can be empty – we can see what fits."

"And if I need to, I can get a roof carrier." I agreed.

"You did have me going over that! When did I get to be so gullible?"

"When were you not? Don't you remember the time…"

But Barb cut me off. "Not now. I've got to go wrap packages."

"What for?" I asked with a frown.

"Christmas! We may not have time to do much when we get there. I've bought all my gifts, but I still haven't wrapped them."

Christmas! I had forgotten Christmas. "We may have to pull a trailer." I sighed.

Chapter 27 — December 22

What makes one place feel like home and another not? Is it only our own sense of security that spreads the blanket of warmth over a town, a neighborhood, a house? Or does something sentient live within the walls and welcome or shun new tenants? I think the deva of the house in Plainview has no strong feelings for me, nor I for it. I know I am a welcome guest, but I am a guest. Perhaps that's why it was so easy to leave.

We had worried about insufficient space in the car, but that problem had been easily solved by a roof carrier to hold all the stuff required by 3 women and 2 dogs traveling at Christmas. We packed in it things we wouldn't need to take into the motels along the way so that we could keep the baggage inside the car to a minimum. We still filled more than half the back seat, but since the top layer was pillows and blankets, whichever of us sat in the back had a very cozy cave for a nap.

Honestly, nothing should have been stressful. We had everything arranged and accounted for well in advance of our departure date. Barb saw to that. But the weather forecasters started to hyperventilate about a Polar Vortex coming down out of Canada into Montana and Wyoming before swooping south to Texas and from there through the middle of the country all the way to New England. And, they predicted, the storm would drop major amounts of snow along the way.

Jo saw the forecast first. She called to consult. "I was just wondering," she began when I cut her off.

"I don't think you had better mention flying," I said sternly.

"No, of course not. It's much too late for that. I was just wondering if we should leave early and try to beat it or wait until it passes."

That was the million-dollar question. We debated. We tried out various scenarios. We finally decided to leave the following day, on the fifteenth. If we got there on the eighteenth, we would just enjoy our longer visit in Plainview.

Our plan was to drive about ten hours each day. We thought we could get to Cleveland the first day, St. Louis on the second, and Plainview on the fourth since we would lay-over in St. Louis for a day while Barb introduced us to her city.

The morning of our departure, we got a later start than we expected since Barb, of all people, had forgotten to shut off the mail delivery. We had to wait until the post office opened before we could get on the road. On such a beautiful day, sunny and in the low fifties, it was difficult to believe we were trying to outrun a storm.

Just outside Albany, we hit rain. It steadily increased in intensity throughout the day. More than once, Barb said, "Thank God it isn't snow." I just wished it wasn't rain.

It was hard to stay calm when the spray from every passing car rendered us momentarily blind. By the time we reached Erie, we were ready to get off the road. Using Jo's list of pet-friendly lodging, we found a comfortable local suite motel. It had a small kitchen area and a pull-out couch in the main room. The other room had two double beds. Both had access to the bathroom.

When we took the dogs out after dinner, the rain had stopped, the wind had picked up, and the temperature felt distinctly colder. Turning on the weather, we discovered that the winds had unexpectedly shifted and Erie was slated for major wintry precipitation: anything between an inch of ice and a foot of snow was possible by morning.

We regrouped again. We were in a nice suite; the restaurant was good; we were warm safe and dry; we would simply stay another day.

And so we did.

Several inches of snow topped a half-inch of ice over most of northwest Pennsylvania and northeast Ohio. The temperatures had dropped into the mid-twenties. We weren't trapped in the car by the side of the road. We were well-fed, warm, and comfortable. A trifle bored, but fine.

During the afternoon of the second day in Erie, Barb's cell phone rang. She looked at the caller-ID in puzzlement. She didn't know the caller. She held the phone warily to her ear as if the stranger at the other end might bite, and said and unsteady, "Hello." She listened, responded "yes" and "no" to apparent questions, and finally said, "Oh, we would love that but we won't be back before the first of the year." After another long pause, she said, "Oh, please do. And thank you for calling."

She lay her phone down and turned to us with a look of triumph. "You'll never guess who that was. Sandy Pine Thomas. Big sister of Sherry Pine." She looked at me for a reaction. I had none. I didn't know who Sherry Pine was. "You know, the Pine kids who grew up in our house."

"Oh, gotcha. What did she say?" I asked.

"She's going to be in Centerbury after Christmas and would like to stop by, meet us, and see what we've done with the house."

"That's good."

"And maybe she can shed some light on the *TRESHUR GUYD*," Barb said. "I can hardly wait!" She nearly clapped her hands in delight.

On the morning of the eighteenth, we finally left Erie. The roads were fine but traffic was heavy. We hoped we could get as far as St. Louis but were prepared to stop short of there if we got too tired. We stopped in Terre Haute, Indiana, in an adequate but not memorable hotel and arrived at the St. Louis arch on the morning of the nineteenth of December.

Barb had agreed to a curtailed visit to her city. She would show us everything important to her during this one day so that we could leave for Plainview the following morning.

She took us by the house she'd lived in, the school where she'd taught, and then seemed to sink into herself.

"Barb, are you OK?" Jo asked her gently.

"Yes. Just feeling odd. I lived here for nearly forty years since college, and I can't think of anything to show you but my house and my school. That feels very sad."

"But Barb, it's not the place. It's the life you lived here that matters. And you can't show us that." Jo said.

"No, I can't. That life is over. And that's really OK, most of the time. But just now, I'm feeling pretty damned nostalgic."

"Then drive around and look at things that mean something to you. Don't worry about us. It's all new to us anyway."

Barb drove to several spots, stopped in front of clothing stores, restaurants, people's homes, and finally announced she was ready to move on. "Thanks for giving me time to lay this place to rest. I didn't do that before I left. And I think I just felt the clinch in my heart release." She wiped a stray tear off the end of her nose. "Now let's find a place to stay tonight."

As we were checking into the motel, I got an unexpected call from Mary Nell Floyd. "Ruth, I think the last time I called you unexpectedly, I told you I needed your help. This time, I think you may need mine."

I was nonplused. "Um, what?" I replied.

"I heard from Belle that you are headed to Plainview. I don't know if you've heard the news today, but most of western Missouri, southern Kansas, and northern Oklahoma are a mess. A big ice storm has stranded thousands, knocked trees down and power out. I hope I caught up with you before you have hit the ice. Where are you?"

"St. Louis."

"OK. Let me do some checking, and I'll get back to you. It'll might be tomorrow morning, but don't leave until you hear from me." She hung up with no goodbye, as was her custom.

I relayed her news to Barb and Jo as I turned on the television. The only thing on any station was scary video of the storm's horrors – trees lying atop houses and roads, abandoned cars scattered over highways – and law enforcement officials tell-ing everyone to stay off the roads in the affected areas.

By the time Mary Nell called again, we were convinced that we'd be spending Christmas in St. Louis. Barb tried to mitigate the disaster with ideas of things we could do there. I appreciated her effort but found little comfort in it.

Mary Nell was as abrupt as usual. "Get a pencil and paper. And a map if you've got one." When I had complied, she laid out a route that took us straight south to Paragould, Arkansas, then across the northern edge of Arkansas to her home in Blue Fork. "It will probably take seven or eight hours and there might be a good bit of traffic if anyone else figures out this detour, but I checked with both Missouri and Arkansas Highway Patrol, and these roads are clear."

She assured me that there would be a hot meal and warm baths in our future. "All you need to do is come," she said before disconnecting.

And so we did.

We followed Mary Nell's directions and found our way easi-ly to Blue Fork and the lane at Floyd's Corners where we turned toward a large, white frame house sitting in the middle of a wide lawn that was surprisingly still green. As soon as we turned to-ward the parking area next to the barn, a blue merle border collie followed by a small girl, blonde braids streaming behind her as she yelled, "Heart, Heart, come back!"

When she saw the car, she skidded to a stop and screeched, "You're here! You're here! Aunt Ruthie! Aunt Barb! You are real-ly here!" She ran to the house, threw open the door, and yelled "They're here! Grandmary, come quick. They're here!"

At a barely reduced pace, she returned to us and introduced us to Heart. As Jo stepped out of the back seat, Bitsy stopped short and demanded, "Well, who are you?"

"Bitsy, don't be rude!" Mary Nell called from the porch. "That's Aunt Ruthie's friend, Miss Jo. And look in the back of the car. There's Sojo and someone else."

Jo walked with Bitsy to the back of the car where she intro-duced Evan as she released both dogs to Bitsy's waiting arms. As she hugged the dogs, Bitsy said, "Heart, Aunt Ruthie and Miss Jo brought you some playmates. This is Sojo and this is Evan. You play nice with them and share your toys." Heart listened carefully to Bitsy before barking and running toward the field, trailing two more barking border collies behind her.

Mary Nell was as good as her promise. She showed us to our warm beds and offered us something to eat. None of us were hungry, but we did accept coffee and tea in Mary Nell's big country kitchen. She showed us the route she had laid out for us to take to Plainview while Bitsy whirled around the central island singing something about an angel.

She came to a stop in front of me, saying excitedly, "Aunt Ruthie, you never saw nothin' prettier than a Christmas Angel. She's all sparkledy white with silver wings. And she can grant wishes with her smile. She gives little children toys and husbands to big women. She's all of the good and none of the bad!"

"Wow!" I said, "where can I find this Christmas Angel?"

"At my play tomorrow night. You can come and see for yourself!"

Barb looked thoughtful, "Hmm, I wonder who might be playing this Christmas Angel. Is it one of your friends?"

"No, Aunt Barb! It's me! I'm the perfect Christmas Angel because I can dance on my toes and twirl my wings. Miss Hunt said so!"

"Ah, I see. Are there other children in the play?"

Bitsy swooped around, twirling her imaginary wings and attempting to spin on her be-sneakered toes. "Oh, sure. Lots. Some are sugarplum fairies, and some are little drummer boys, and some are snowflakes, and some are reindeer. But there's only one Christmas Angel – me! And you can come see me, can't you? PLEASE! And Aunt Ruthie and Miss Jo can come, too. Oh, PLEASE!"

Barb prevaricated, "It's very nice of you to ask us, Bitsy, and it's very tempting, but I need to talk it over with Ruth and Jo. And we need to make sure that your Grandmary doesn't object."

Bitsy threw herself at Mary Nell, grabbing her by the neck. "Grandmary, you don't ject do you?"

Mary Nell had been talking with Jo and not paying attention to Bitsy's theatrics. "I don't what, Bits?"

"Ject," she repeated.

"Ject? I don't know what you mean."

"Ject, Grandmary! You don't ject to Aunt Barb and Aunt Ruthie and Miss Jo coming to see the Christmas Angel, do you?"

"Oh," Mary Nell smiled, "no, I don't object. In fact I think that's a very good idea. Then Walter could show you around Blue Fork in the morning. He's dying to."

We promised Bitsy that we'd think about it and let her know.

"Don't think too hard," she warned, "it can make your hair fall out. That's what happened to Gramps."

After a big dinner of Walter's special 3-Alarm Chili with all the trimmings, Betty and Buck arrived to pick up Bitsy. Betty's copper-colored hair and athletic build complemented Buck's sandy-toned cowboy good looks. They made a handsome couple, brought together by a common love of good food and Walter Floyd.

"It's so nice to meet you, Betty," Barb told her. "You know I fell in love with your daughter last summer."

"It was mutual. It was 'Aunt Barb this' and 'Aunt Ruthie that' for weeks after she got home. Oh, that reminds me, did you ever find any more treasure?"

As Barb filled Betty in about the *TRESHUR GUYD*, I chatted with Buck. He was justifiably proud of the organic produce he was growing in the bank of greenhouses he pointed out to me, just down the lane from the barn. "Walter gave me a chance," he told me, "and I plan to make sure he doesn't regret it."

In the end, we stayed an extra day. We could hear Bitsy's whoop through the phone when Mary Nell told her. And Walter was nearly as excited about showing us his town.

Walter's tour included stops at Betty's Main Street Cafe, and Grandpa's Greens, the organic produce market managed by Betty's father and stocked by Buck's produce. Blue Fork was a thriving little town with many active businesses and services. Walter was justifiably proud of it. He had helped to bring it back from near ghost-town status to a bustling community by giving low-interest loans to entrepreneurs and by renovating business and residential spaces to make them more appealing to the young professionals he was attempting to attract.

We had lunch at Betty's cafe where we were treated to well-cooked organic foods that originated in her father's market and in Buck's greenhouses.

Sated, we dozed on the way back to Floyd's Corners but managed to wake up enough to play with the dogs and enjoy the sunny weather that seemed to mock the still-devastated area not many miles north of us.

Mary Nell had tea and cookies for us when we came inside. She was ready for a "chin wag" she said with a sardonic smile. Her Rainbow Coalition t-shirt and lavender socks sticking out the toes of battered Birkenstocks were at odds with the hillbilly idioms she played with.

"So, Jo, have you moved to Vermont, too?" she asked after making sure we were all well-tended.

"No, not yet. I'm trying it out," Jo answered. "But I just may make it permanent if I can work everything out in Plainview."

"I understand the beauty of the setting, and I approve of the politics of Vermont. But what makes it attractive to you? Besides Ruth's presence, of course."

"I've been thinking about that quite a bit lately," Jo replied. "Except for Ruth whom I've known since high school, nobody there knows anything about me except what I show them right now. There's something so freeing about not lugging around past versions of yourself or trying to live up to expectations that those past versions generated."

She sipped her tea. "I know that sounds like I have something to hide – no, I am not an escaped convict – but I hid behind a facade in Plainview for more than thirty years. When I finally decided to show my true face, not everyone liked it. I screwed with their expectations. In Centerbury, nobody has any expectations. I can be who I am unapologetically."

Mary Nell leaned her cheek on her fist. "I wonder if Belle feels like that now"

Jo reached across the table and patted Mary Nell's hand. "I know she does. She spent a lot of years trying to keep her daughter safe by staying away from her. She told me that once the secret was out, she nearly collapsed from the lack of the burden. She didn't know how to walk without carrying that weight."

Mary Nell sniffed and swallowed. "I had to let go a bundle of hurt and anger, too. The oddest thing is that I didn't know I was carrying it."

"Not so odd. Most of us don't feel the weight of our protective clothing until we take it off. The lightness of our being is breathtaking," Jo said softly.

I wiggled uncomfortably in my chair. "So," I said, shifting topics abruptly, "what time is the shindig tonight?"

Everyone looked at me in surprise. Mary Nell shifted gears first. "At 6:30. I thought we'd eat afterwards. It will only last about an hour."

Barb studied me with a frown before saying, "I am so full from Betty's lunch and these wonderful cookies, I could probably make it until 7:30 tomorrow night." She stood up, placed her hand on my shoulder, and said, "I think I'm going to rest a little while before the play."

Mary Nell let out a little gasp. "Damn! The play. I forgot to send the halo home with Bitsy." She dashed into the living room to locate the missing accessory.

Jo looked at me carefully as I fiddled with my mug. "What's going on, Ruth?"

"Oh, I just started thinking about Bitsy and the play. That's all."

Jo just watched me.

"OK, I'm not really into soul-baring right now." I stood up and turned toward the doorway.

"Well, if you ever do get into it, I'll be around." Jo smiled and took a final sip of tea.

The auditorium at the primary school was filled to capacity. Christmas songs and carols were playing over the speakers. At 6:30 promptly, Miss Hunt, Bitsy's teacher, announced that this year, the school was presenting a living Christmas Tree.

The curtains opened on a 4-tier riser bathed in green light. The music shifted to "The Little Drummer Boy" and around 15 little drummer boys in blue coats carrying red drums marched out and positioned themselves on the floor and the riser. Most of them were scattered on the floor, fewer on the lowest level of the riser, fewer still on the second level, only two on the third level and none on top. After they were all positioned, they sang a verse of their song.

Next out were the sugarplum fairies in lavender tutus with gossamer wings stepping lightly to the Tchaikovsky dance of the same name. After they positioned themselves among the drummers, they twirled in place to their song.

The snowflakes, in dark blue leotards with sparkling white hexagons attached to their chests, arrived to "Let It Snow." They scattered out among the others and bounced up and down in a simulated blizzard.

"Rudolph the Red Nosed Reindeer" introduced the red-nosed antlered crew who pranced across the stage and filled in the final gaps of the riser. Their rendition of the classic tune was more enthusiastic than musical.

The lights on the stage dimmed and a single spot shone at the center of the empty top riser. Suddenly, a little voice sang out "Christmas Angel, You're so lovely, and you top our little tree so fine. For your halo and your silver wings can really shine!" It was sung to the tune of "Johnny Angel" by none other than our Bitsy who had somehow appeared at the top of the decorated living tree.

Miss Hunt reappeared and directed the entire tree in a chorus of "We Wish You a Merry Christmas." It was a rousing success.

We found Bitsy afterwards to hug, praise, thank, and bid farewell. The next morning we would leave for our final destination.

We waved and honked as we drove out of the driveway and turned the car to the west. Our stay in Blue Fork had been pleasant, but we were ready for Plainview.

Now, Barb, Sojo and I were safely ensconced in my old room in the big house Janie had bought in Plainview. Jo was at her own house down the road with her sister and Evan. We were at journey's end, and we were tired.

It had been a nerve-wracking trip although not a dangerous one. We had had no car trouble that required the use of flares. We did not get stranded in a snow-drift and have to subsist on Hershey bars and peanut butter crackers while huddled with the dogs under insufficient blankets. But we were very happy to have arrived at our destination with nowhere to travel the next morning.

Chapter 28 — December 23

Janie had dressed the house to the nines in holiday garb: evergreen boughs, wreaths, candles, Santas, trees, bells, angels, crèches, ribbons, candy canes, and snowmen everywhere. There was even a dove sitting on a ball of mistletoe in my bathroom! She must have hit a hell of a sale at some Christmas store.

Never one to do things by halves, she had outdone even herself on Christmas goodies. She had fudge, divinity, candy cane cupcakes, popcorn balls, filled candy, and every kind of decorated cookie imaginable. I told her I would gain weight just from breathing in all the sugar in the air.

Jake was wound up so tight he spun. He couldn't decide whether to beg for cookies; run with Sojo and his dog, Oliver; show me his new treasures — birds' nests and turtle shells topped the list; or drag Barb through all his favorite places in the house and his fort. He flitted between all of the above with a manic intensity that was "sugar-charged and not very healthy" according to his mother.

After quietly watching his frantic activity for several minutes, Win called him. "Jake, I could use some help with the firewood. Can you do that?"

Jake screeched to a halt. He smiled and said sweetly, "Sure, Daddy Bear," as he slipped his hand into Win's gigantic one.

With their departure, the noise level in the house dropped to as-yet unheard levels. Janie sighed and dropped into a chair. "He wears me out. Thank goodness he adores Win. All it takes is a soft word from 'Daddy Bear' and he's a different child."

I ruffled her dark curls, "You're a different child, too. You're still radiant after a year of marriage. It's still good?"

Janie nodded happily, "It's all good! But, oh, I do miss you terribly! I hope you're happy enough in Vermont to justify forsaking me!"

"You look forsaken," I cocked my head and studied her. "Actually, you look a little round. Have you gained weight?"

Janie blushed, "Well, um, I was waiting for the right time to tell you, but...."

"You're pregnant!" I interrupted. "You are, aren't you?"

Janie nodded. I hugged her. Barb hugged her. We all hugged each other.

"Have you told Jake yet?" Barb asked.

"No, not yet. I want to make it special. I don't know if I want to tie it all up with Christmas. But I can't figure out what I want to do. Any ideas?"

Barb promised to think about it. I only wanted my questions answered. "When are you due? What does Win think? Who have you told? Are you feeling OK?"

When I stopped, Janie grinned and said, "June, ecstatic, nobody, perfect."

By then I'd forgotten what I'd asked. But June had to be when. "June! That's a great time. I'll come stay with you a couple of weeks when she's born if you'd like me to."

Janie jumped up wrapped her arms around my neck. "I was hoping you'd say that. I know I will need some help, particularly with Jake. I could probably hire one of the local care givers, but you are my number one choice. Oh! I am so happy!" She danced me around the room, giggling. I giggled with her. Since she was a little girl, her infectious laugh always got me going.

Barb watched us with a smile. "I guess I'll have to get out my knitting needles."

"You knit?" I said in astonishment. "I've never seen you knit."

Barb said flatly, "You've never seen me do many things I do quite well."

"I guess that's true," I conceded. "But I *have* seen you do many things quite well and some not so well."

"I'll give you that," Barb nodded. "But I really can knit. Would you like a blanket, Janie? What color?"

"Oh, Barb, I would love to have a blanket. Either yellow or pale green, I guess, since I don't know the sex. And I'm not really into the pink and blue thing anyway. Just something soft and sweet," her entire face softened as she spoke.

"I've got until June? Surely I can finish a blanket by then. Something soft and sweet coming up."

Janie squeezed her hand. "Thanks, Barb. Oh, hey, I'd like to show you two what I'm working on. Come back to my studio."

Janie's studio had been only partially finished when she bought the house, but Win had put his building skills to good use. Now the big room with six windows had not only sheetrock but also cork sheets on all the walls. He'd added overhead lights, a window unit air conditioner, and a small wood-burning stove, making this room ready for any season. I looked around in pleasure. This was a room where Janie could work.

And work she had. Along one wall she had tacked up storyboards for a book she was illustrating. It was another Wee Folk adventure. In this one, the Wee Folk were looking for treasure in an old house. "See, you've inspired me," she said.

Barb whispered loudly, "Where do they find the treasure? I really need to know."

"Damn!" Janie said. "I was hoping you'd tell me."

Barb laughed and told Janie about the *TRESHUR GUYD* we had found, all the places we had looked, and the upcoming visit of Sandy Pine Thomas. "I have high hopes she'll know something," Barb concluded.

"Promise to let me know. I want to do something surprising with my treasure, but I can't think of anything."

I said dryly, "You live in Plainview. You should do the Purloined Letter bit."

Janie frowned at me for several beats. "Oh, plain view. Got it."

"Hmm," Barb said. "I've been so busy looking for secret hiding places, I didn't think about that."

"Barb, as much scouring over our houses as we have done, don't you think we'd have seen anything obvious by now?"

Barb reached in her pocket for her ever-present notebook and pen and began writing furiously. Janie watched her in awe. "Wow, she must have come up with something." As she spoke, she unconsciously sketched what looked like a rudimentary map on the brown paper that covered the tables. "And you know what, so have I! I think I can camouflage this map in the lines and cracks of the cellar wall." She walked to the painting of the Wee Folk searching for gold in the cellar. With only a few deft strokes of her oil pastel crayon, she had hidden her map in the stone wall. "I think that will work. Thanks, you two."

I could barely find it and I knew it was there.

Barb looked stunned. "Do you think that might be it? I never thought to look. I'm going to call Jack and ask him if he'd go photograph our cellar walls and email the photos to me."

"Barb, really?" I asked.

She deflated. "Oh, no, of course not. It's Christmas. I'll wait until the 26th."

I raised both eyebrows and cocked my head.

"OK. I'll wait until we get home and look myself." She sighed, "Ruth, you just have no sense of adventure."

Janie hooted, "Oh, tell her about the time you got lost in the red-light district of Shanghai. Or what about the runaway train in Wuxi"

"Enough, Missy. Barb doesn't care about all of that."

"How can you possibly say that? I don't *know* about all of that. You haven't told me. I thought you were some sort of staid corporate employee all those years not some foreign adventuress!" Barb paused for air. "Janie, we need to talk."

Chapter 29 — December 26

Boxing Day. A legal holiday in Canada, the UK, and a few other places. Nobody I know seems to know why except that traditionally it entailed giving gifts to those of a lower social class. It has evolved into a day to hit the after-Christmas sales and watch football. Not surprising. Christmas has evolved from pagan winter celebrations, Saturnalia, and other winter solstice festivals into a roiling mass of consumerism. Where are the Puritans when we need them to cancel Christmas again?

Jake received so many presents that he exhausted himself trying to decide which to play with first. I plead guilty to adding to his frenzy. My excuse is that it's fun to give presents when the recipient squeals with glee. Stokes the ego, I guess. With adults, you generally have to settle for nothing more than a bright smile and a sincere "thank you".

I was impressed with Win's gifts. He obviously chose them with care. They reflected both his innate kindness and his wry sense of humor. He got his share of bright smiles.

He gave me a canvas satchel onto which he had stenciled "Pilgrimage Pouch." In it were a box of the extra-fine roller ball pens and four of the Black 'n Red notebooks that I favor. I laughed aloud at his allusion to my Tales and hugged him for noticing the tools I used.

Janie had invited Sally, Belle, Jo and her sister, Ellen, and Gerry Krane to dinner. Gerry was unavailable, but everyone else arrived bearing gifts and food. It was a joyful feast – everyone talking, dogs barking, and Jake running from gift to gift, room to room, dog to dog until he fell into a pile on a cushion in front of the fireplace. Oliver and Sojo stood guard.

After coffee and dessert, we settled around the now-empty table to talk. Jo surprised everyone with her announcement, "I'm going to close the diner."

"Oh, no!" Janie interrupted. "There's nowhere else to eat for 30 miles, and it's not any good."

"Wait," Jo said, holding up palm, "I'm going to close it for a couple of weeks so that Ellen can have a vacation. She'll ride back to Vermont with me, see what I love about it, and fly back to Wichita on January 12. I was wondering if any of you could pick her up from the airport."

Four hands shot into the air accompanied by a chorus of "I can!"

Jo leaned back in her chair, eyes wide. "Win, you have a job with regular hours. You can't just up and drive to Wichita."

Win pursed his lips and nodded. "You ever hear of vacation?" He nodded again. "Besides, I want to go to Wichita. There's a garden shop there that specializes in shade plants. I want to see what they'll have for me in the Spring. I have a whole new yard to landscape now, you know." He turned his thousand-watt smile on Janie.

She winked at him then declared, "I want to go, too. I heard about a new art supply store over by Wichita State. I like to be able to look at and touch brushes and paper before I buy them."

"Well, dang!" Sally blurted. "I need to go look for new video equipment. I've decided to create some supplementary training videos for new handlers. I think it can be beneficial in reinforcing bloodhound man-trailing exercises."

Belle said quietly, "Bull hockey. You know you want to go to that massage therapist you read about who's working on regenerating muscle tissue caused by old injuries. I saw you tearing out that article and putting on your desk. God knows how you'll ever find it again."

Sally squinted at Belle, "Hmph. Well why do you want to go to Wichita?"

"Ship a dog to Mexico. It's the closest place with jets that have pet-friendly cargo areas. You know that new, whachacallit airline."

"Well," Win said looking over the volunteers, "I've got a big van. We would all fit. Even have room to take a dog and bring back Ellen and her luggage."

On hearing her name, Ellen jerked out of her stunned silence. "Oh, my goodness, I've never had such a welcome home committee before in my entire life even though I realize you all have other reasons to go to Wichita it will still feel like a welcome when you pick me up at the airport and bring me back to Plainview where I'm beginning to feel at home even though I'm living in a different place and have a different job I still know all of you!" She beamed at each of us.

Barb's jaw dropped half-way through the soliloquy. I nudged her to close her mouth and whispered to her, "Later."

Jo noticed our interaction and accompanied her rueful smile with a slight shrug. "Well, OK, then," she said turning to Win. "I'll book her flight tomorrow and let you know the details. Would you prefer she arrive in the late afternoon?" She noted the heads nodding and continued, "Good. I'll let you know what I come up with."

"And thank you so much for making this possible for me since I've never been east of the Mississippi, or really east of Little Rock, before, let alone north nearly to Canada where I'm sure it's colder than I've ever been in my life so I'll need to get warm clothes before we go, OK, Jo?" Ellen asked expectantly.

Jo answered, "Sure, Ellen. We'll go shopping before we leave here."

"I'm going to Enid this week to show Barb around. You two want to come with us?" I asked.

"I'm not sure I've ever shopped in Enid though I did go there once but I think the shops were closed or was that Ponca City or maybe Tulsa, I really can't remember."

Jo rolled her eyes in my direction. "Yes," she said, "that'll be great."

Ellen began another interminable sentence about her availability based on when Jo wanted to keep the diner open, but I tuned out. Something was making Ellen very nervous. She could be damn-near terse when she felt comfortable in a situation.

"Ellen," I interrupted her, "have you ever flown before?"

"No, not to say 'flown' though I was once in an airplane that landed in Daddy's field over in Arkansas and I wanted so much to fly off with that cute pilot but his engine had problems and I had to go to school and wouldn't you know it, he got his plane fixed and was gone before I got home."

"Oh," Jo said to me. "I hadn't thought of that. Are you nervous about flying, Ellen?"

"Well, nervous might be too strong but I am not completely comfortable with the idea of being disconnected from earth for several hours and at the mercy of a stranger whose capabilities I can only take on faith, however it will be lovely to have a welcoming committee to pick me up assuming we do land."

Ellen took a large swallow of tea. I imagine her throat would get dry.

"We'll work on it," I told the future welcoming committee.

The party broke up soon afterward. All of us were exhausted. I had never before fully appreciated how difficult listening could be.

Boxing Day was bright and clear. Christmas and all the hubbub was over, and I was glad of it. I was ready to head home to Vermont. But first I wanted to see Gerry Krane and talk with her about my Tales. I missed having her as my Proofing Pal. I was hoping we could renew that relationship electronically. After all, we didn't have to be in the same neighborhood to share our writing with each other.

When I called Gerry, she suggested I come see her that afternoon. Barb declined to go, preferring to stay in and read the new Louise Penny novel that Jo had given her.

Gerry welcomed me with a hug, and her dog, Jess, made Sojo welcome with a reciprocal butt-sniff. Gerry's dining table was covered with wadded balls of paper, books propped open with cans of fruit and dog food, stacks of printed pages, and the expected laptop. I grinned at the mess. "Looks like you've been busy. How's the book coming?"

"Oh, Ruth! I'm stuck. I think some of what I've written is really good, but now I've hit a quandary."

"I didn't know you could hit them."

"Oh, yeah." She ran her hands through her long red hair. "You can hit them, be stuck in them, and die struggling in them."

She looked so forlorn I put an arm around her shoulder and squeezed. "What's the quandary?"

"Remember when I started this project? I was so jazzed about Miss Velma Lee. I just knew I could write a wonderful novel based on her journal and her sayin's. But I've just found something about her that would shock everyone in town. And I don't know what to do about it. Dammit! I wish I hadn't found it."

"Didn't she say, 'You can't forget something you never knew'?" I asked.

"Well, yes. So are you saying I should forget it?"

"Let me ask you this: is it necessary to know the secret to understand Miss Velma Lee?"

"It adds another layer to her. It helps you see what turned her into the manners maven she became," she said thoughtfully.

"OK. Then what damage will your revelation do?"

"It'll knock her off that pedestal she's been on for a hundred years."

"Is that harmful?"

Gerry fiddled with a pen, tapping her teeth with its top. "Um, no. In fact it might be helpful."

"There's your answer then." I leaned back in the chair and cocked my head. "So what's the secret?"

"Did you just solve my problem or manipulate me into telling you the secret?"

I raised an eyebrow. "Does it have to be one or the other?"

Gerry laughed. "No. It can be both." Her green eyes twinkled. "Miss Velma Lee Lewis did not attend the Mansfield Finishing School for Young Women. She ran off with a traveling salesman. They never married. In fact, he disappeared after about a year. She ended up pregnant and alone. She eventually wrote her father. Dr. Lewis arranged for a friend from medical school to take care of his pregnant daughter and adopt out the resultant child. The baby, a girl, was adopted by a family named Mansfield in St. Louis. Their family ran a finishing school. Thus was hatched the big lie that colored the rest of Miss Velma Lee's life."

"Wow! That's quite a story! How did you discover it?"

"Digging through old records of the Mansfield school. They're now housed in the public library. Unbelievably, letters from Dr. Lewis' friend, Dr. Thom Smith, to Mrs. Mansfield arranging the adoption were in the very dusty archives. I sneezed for weeks."

"How can you contemplate not telling that story?" I asked a little sharply.

"I'll destroy her reputation!" Gerry wailed.

"Gerry Krane! This is not 1917! You will not destroy her reputation. If anything, you'll enhance it. Everyone loves stories of people getting themselves back up after a fall."

Gerry sighed. "I guess you're right." She tapped her teeth with her pen again. "I'll have to recast the introduction. Or maybe just reveal it in the epilogue. But that feels like cheating. I guess I'll have to insert it chronologically and....Oh, I'm sorry, Ruth. You got my mind churning."

"Good. I'm going to leave and let you churn away. It was great to see you!" I gathered up my coat and satchel and prepared to leave.

"Oh, no, wait! I haven't asked you about your writing, or how you like Vermont or how you're doing with your agility dog. Oh, don't leave yet!" She grabbed my arm.

"I'll see you before we leave. Write about the real Miss Velma Lee," I disengaged her hand, squeezed it, called Sojo, and left. It was an unexpected treat to be able to help Gerry solve a problem.

Chapter 30 — December 31

I had been a whirlwind of activity for the past few days. I visited, again, all my friends. I took Barb to eat at Jo's diner and to Enid shopping, and I played with Jake, Oliver, and Sojo until I was stiff from sitting in the "fort" and sore from throwing balls and Frisbees.

We had decided to leave in time to see the New Year in from Vermont. And luckily, the weather cooperated. Everything was clear for our entire route.

On the morning of the 29th, we said our goodbyes, hugged Jake numerous times and everyone else at least once. We told Jo to drive carefully and Ellen to keep her awake. Jo gave me a look. I had no doubt Ellen could keep her awake with endless chatter. We loaded Sojo in her crate. Oliver, Evan, and Jess barked their farewells. Sojo responded with her roo-roo-roo as we drove away.

The trip home was uneventful if long. The weather was clear, the roads were clear. We had no problems with food, fuel, lodging or the car. It was perfectly boring until we got to St. Louis.

When we first saw the Arch, Barb began a story. "Ben loved the Arch. He made pilgrimages to it nearly every month for over forty years. He had thousands of photographs, from every possible angle, in every possible weather and every possible light condition. He had the moon rising under the Arch, fireworks under the Arch, flags under the Arch, and I think a big kite under the arch.

"He started his devotion when the arch was being erected in the mid 1960's. He was there for the dedication in '68. He was in high school. Most of his friends were disdainful, at least out loud, about the amazing structure, but Ben never pretended indifference. It was love at first sight.

"He could quote all the stats: how much stainless steel it took – hint, the most of any structure in the world – how much concrete, the size of its cross-section, its height and span – the same – and the geometry of it. It's a catenary not a parabola."

She paused and looked out the window, smiling at the silver triangle arching upward, reflected in the Mississippi River. "I really need to do something with Ben's collection. Donate it to the city, or something. I just haven't been able to face it. Maybe holding on to it lets me hang on to a piece of Ben." She cleared her throat and sniffed a little. Then turned around to look out the back window as the Arch disappeared behind us.

After a few minutes of silence, I said, "You don't talk much about Ben. I think this is the first time I've heard you mention him."

"I figured you didn't want to hear."

"Why would you think that?"

"Because you never talk about anything personal."

"What?" I was shocked. "I talk to you all the time."

"Do you?" Barb asked quietly.

I didn't reply. I couldn't think of anything to say.

The next morning at breakfast, if you want to call a stale donut and a cup of weak coffee "breakfast", I got a text message from Gerry. She had figured out how to incorporate the new information about Miss Velma Lee into her book. "Much improved. Book and me. Thx," she had written.

I said aloud, "That's great!"

"What?" Barb looked up from reading an abandoned 2-day old newspaper.

"Oh, Gerry figured out how to solve the problem with her book." I typed a congratulatory text into my phone as I spoke.

When I looked up, Barb was studying me. She shook her head slightly and returned to reading her newspaper.

"What?" I asked.

"Nothing," she sighed, "nothing at all."

After we got on the road, I decided to tell Barb about Miss Velma Lee. Barb listened intently. She laughed with me as I told her some of my favorite "sayin's" – "Never dust your tabletops after dark" and "Only spit in moving water or deep leaves" topped my list.

I described how Janie had used Miss Velma Lee's sayin's to get to know the people in Plainview during the party she threw. She got everyone to write down their favorite. Everyone over the age of 20 knew Miss Velma Lee.

"That was very clever," Barb remarked. "That Janie's a keeper!"

"Yep. And so's Win. I'm lucky to have those two! Anyway, Miss Velma Lee always presented herself as the arbitrator of good manners. Everyone in Plainview believed her. So when Gerry discovered that the paragon of virtue had a past, she couldn't imagine revealing it. I helped her realize that knowing all the information about Miss Velma Lee made her more human. It would help people relate to her, understand her, empathize with her. And probably keep her from being nothing but a joke to the younger generation."

Barb chewed her bottom lip for a few minutes before saying, "It's amazing how clear-eyed we can be about other people."

I nearly swerved into the right lane as I turned to look at her. "What do you mean?"

"Nothing." She sighed. "Not a thing."

For the remainder of the drive, I told amusing stories about my travels in Asia and Barb reciprocated with teacher mishaps and student bloopers. We kept it light. We laughed together, reminisced about college days, and played I-wonder-what-she's-doing-now, devising careers for old sorority sisters. The best was

Barb's description of the current life of the 1972 campus tramp, Donita Strong.

"After she left school," Barb began, "she took a job as a bartender at a strip joint. It was there she met Steven Mann, a good-looking, quick-thinking, fast-talking con man with an eye for a quick buck, legally obtained or not. He could charm the panties off anyone. Donita was no challenge. She never wore panties. But something about her caught his attention and he decided he needed her to help him fulfill his dreams. He wanted to be a faith healer, and he decided he needed a wife to be successful in his chosen career.

"He married Donita. They made a great team. Together they conducted tent revivals all over the South, making millions of dollars from their donations and sales of CDs, videos, books, and snake oil.

"Steven died suddenly, leaving her with a money-making machine but no machine operator. She flipped around, trying to decide what to do with herself, when one of her supporters convinced her to run for an open Congressional seat in Mississippi, on the Tea Party ticket.

"Her campaign slogan is 'Donita Strong Mann — when You've Got a Strong Woman!' And she still doesn't wear underpants."

I howled, picturing old skuzzy Donita as a perfectly coifed politician kissing babies and shaking hands. "You win! I can't compete with that."

We were still laughing and further elaborating on Donita's campaign when we pulled into the driveway of our houses. Sojo sang roo-roo-roo as she jumped out of the car and ran in circles in her backyard.

I picked up voice mail from my land line and found a message from Janet Maples, of all people, inviting us to her New Year's Eve party. I was delighted to be able to reply with the truth: we just got home and were too tired to stay up to see the New Year in.

I had just hung up from leaving that message when Barb came in, still holding her phone in her hand.

"I left regrets for Janet Maples," I told her.

"What for?"

"The party tonight. I told her we were too tired to go. Didn't she invite you?"

"I don't know. I haven't checked all my messages. The first one was too exciting. Sandy Pine Thomas is coming over tomorrow around eleven, on her way to the airport in Albany. I'm so glad we got home in time to meet her."

"Me, too. I'm eager to find out what she knows. But remember, she never lived here as an adult. All her memories will be from childhood."

"I know. But I have a feeling that she has the key I need." She stopped short. "Key. My God, what have I done with that key? Remember, it was with that tobacco tin that had the article about the map. I don't think I put the key back in the tin. Oh, I have to find it. I'm going to go look for it then go to bed. I'm exhausted. Happy New Year!" she said as she disappeared through the passageway.

I sighed and dropped into my recliner. "At least I've got you, Soj. Happy New Year, girl."

"Roo-roo-roo," she replied.

Chapter 31 — January 1

The sun sets; the sun rises. A year dies; a year is born.
Chief Broom says they speed up the clocks when you're having fun and slow them down when you're miserable. My clock ran fast this year.
Ring out the old; ring in the new.
The queen is dead. Long live the queen!

Sandy Pine Thomas rang the bell promptly at eleven. I'm not sure what I expected, but she was not it. She was barely five feet tall, sapling-thin, with chopped-off multi-colored hair and wide blue eyes. Her clothes were covered with blobs of color. As she extended her hand to shake mine, I noticed her palm was green. An elf in motley.

"Wow!" she said, Her head swiveled as she tried to see everything at once. "You've been busy! I like the plain walls. I was after Mama for years to get rid of her big floral wallpaper, but she loved it." She took a deep breath that ended with a sigh. "God, Mama loved this house. When Daddy moved us here from Ontario, Mama was miserable until she found this house. It is so strange for her not to be here. I'm sorry. I think I'm babbling. Do you mind if I sit down? Oh, don't worry," she pointed to her pants, "the paint's dry."

"Oh, of course. Please have a seat. Would you like some coffee or tea?" I asked.

"Coffee would be heaven. Thank you." She leaned back and looked over the room. She smiled as she examined the fireplace, then took another deep breath.

Barb tilted her head toward the kitchen. I nodded slightly and went in to get the coffee. Barb followed, telling Sandy we would give her a minute to get her bearings.

As we brewed coffee and assembled a tray with cups and cookies, Barb whispered, "Well, she's not what I expected."

"No joke. Did you see her green hand?" I asked.

"Shh." Barb squeezed her lips together, trying to contain a giggle.

When we returned to the living room, Sandy was photographing the room. "I hope you don't mind, but I promised photos to my sisters. And I thought I might try to paint that fireplace. I'm not sure. I don't usually do interiors. But I can almost see it. Dream-like. Painting memories in a solid frame. Oh, sorry. I'm babbling again."

As she drank her coffee, she asked us about why we'd bought the house and how we liked living in it. "You know, we never lived in the workshop – your house, Barb. We always kept it rented. Had some interesting tenants. The worst was my sixth-grade teacher. Oh, she was nice enough, but imagine living so close to your teacher! Now what kind of job did you have, Barb?"

"I was a teacher," Barb said dryly.

"Oh. My ex-husband always told me I have foot-in-mouth disease."

"It's OK. I know what you meant. Now would you like a little tour?"

Sandy took hundreds of photos as we walked through first Barb's house then mine. She even photographed the inside of my closet.

"Look here," she directed, lighting the back corner with the flashlight on her cell phone. "Had you noticed that before?" Just above the baseboard, written in red crayon, was a heart and the phrase "Sandy Loves Johnny Huggins." She laughed. "I must have been about twelve when I wrote that. I wondered if it had been covered over."

"I haven't painted inside the closets yet. But when I do, I'll leave it," I promised.

After the tour, Barb brought out all the treasures we had found: the tobacco tins, the wooden box, the bag of gold, the newspaper articles, the brass key, and the cigar box with the *TRESHUR GUYD* inside. She spread them on the coffee table in front of Sandy.

"I see you found them. Oh, gosh! I had forgotten about the *TRESHUR GUYD*. Susie wrote that. She must have been about six. We had a club. I was president – I was nine – and Susie was secretary. I can't remember what Sherry was. She was just a baby."

Barb was stunned. "You found all these things?" She swept her hand across the table. "Then, what? Put them back?"

"Sure," Sandy replied. "We didn't need them. The fun was finding them. I think I was about fifteen when we put everything back."

I picked up the bag of little gold nuggets. "Did you know this is real gold? It's worth a few hundred dollars."

"Really? No, we just thought it was another prize we had to find in the treasure hunt."

"Did your parents know about the treasure hunt?" Barb asked.

"No way. Mama would have been angry we didn't include her. She loved puzzles; she would have taken over. We wanted to do this ourselves."

I nodded. "What's the key for? Are we missing its box?" I held up the brass key tied with the red ribbon.

Sandy took it and grinned. "That's the key I lost! It was to an old jewelry box I had. Daddy had to break it open after I lost the key. I quit using it since I couldn't keep my sisters out of it without the lock. Where was it?"

"In the tobacco tin that had the article about the treasure map of the cemetery," Barb replied.

"I'll bet Sherry hid it there. She was always trying to get into my jewelry box. I hid the key, but she must have found it. She was such a pest!"

"But, but," Barb stammered. "I'm having trouble getting my arms around this. You girls found all these things, treasures, and then put them back? Who hid them in the first place?"

"Oh," Sandy said with glee, "you haven't found the last one yet." She grinned mischievously, enhancing her resemblance to an elf. "I can't tell you. You'll have to find it yourselves. Oh, this is great! Wait 'til I tell the girls!" She chuckled as she snapped photos of the articles on the table.

Barb huffed. "Are you sure you won't tell me?"

Sandy shook her head. "No can do."

I interrupted the standoff. "More coffee?"

"I'd love some," Sandy said. "I was out painting since early this morning and I didn't take time to get another cup. I tend to lose track of time, hunger, thirst, and everything else when I'm painting."

"You paint in oil?" I asked, looking pointedly at her pants.

"Yep. Oh, I forgot to ask, is it OK if I change here before I go to the airport? I'm not sure what the TSA would make of these pants."

"Of course, you can. What do you paint?" Barb asked.

"Landscapes. Outdoors – plein air. I like getting down here to paint the places I remember as a kid."

"Where do you live now?" I said.

"Oh, up in the Northeast Kingdom. Little village in the middle of nowhere that has astonishing views. It's about a four-and-a-half-hour drive, so I don't get down here very often."

"And you're going to fly home?" Barb asked with a frown.

"No, I'm flying to Arizona. There's a big plein air event in the dessert. I'm doing the Paint Out and I have a piece in the show." She glanced at her watch. "I better get moving. I'll get my clothes and change."

As she changed clothes, Barb said "What's a Paint Out?"

I shrugged. I'd look it up later.

Sandy returned looking more presentable if still green-handed. "I'm sorry I have to leave so quickly, but I really do need to go." She took a last look around the living room, and said

"Thank you so much for letting me see what you've done with this old place. I think Mama would approve."

I walked her to the door. As she climbed into her car she yelled, "Let me know when you find the last treasure."

Barb moved the found objects around on the table. She looked so crestfallen I had to laugh.

"Why so glum, chum?" I asked her. "You still have a table full of treasures and another one to find."

"Oh, I don't know. I guess I just thought there might be something really valuable. That we'd be rich. I'm just a little disappointed." She sighed.

"I'm not. I'm intrigued. Why would those kids put everything back? There's still a mystery to solve. It's just not the one we thought it was."

Barb nodded and lifted her coffee cup. "So here's to a fresh start. Happy New Year!"

Chapter 32 — January 3

I couldn't stop thinking about Barb's comments to me during our drive home from Oklahoma. Was I really as uncommunicative as she suggested?

I tried to think of times when I had been forthcoming about my feelings, my writing, or anything. I wriggled uncomfortably inside my skin. I needed to do something different. It was January 3, but I thought it wasn't too late for a resolution.

I picked up my iPad, planning to look at my email or play a game of solitaire to distract myself from uncomfortable thoughts, when I had an idea. I typed *ruthwelborne.com* in the browser search box. Then I went in search of Barb. I wasn't ready to share the Tales, but my blog was already public.

When I handed her the iPad, she looked at the screen then at me in surprise. She started to say something but stopped herself. She looked back at my blog. "I'll read this with interest," she said mildly.

I smiled to myself and left her alone to read. That went better than I had expected.

Jo called mid-morning and said they would be arriving in the early afternoon. "We've been leading a huge storm all the way from Kansas. I think we are still about eight to ten hours ahead of it."

"I'm glad you called. We were wondering where you were. Plan to come here for dinner tonight. You'll be too tired to cook. And I'll go to the store and get you in enough provisions to last a couple of days so you won't have to shop immediately."

"Oh, thanks. That would be great. If you go by my house, would you turn the heat up, too. I think it's set at fifty degrees. Ellen will not like that!"

"Will do. Drive safely. See you soon."

I went to tell Barb about Jo's call and found her sitting in the living room, still holding my iPad. "Oh, Ruth, you write beautifully. You need to do more of it."

"Thanks. I'm working on it. I'm making progress on my Tales. I've got ten written. I still think I'll go for twelve." I raised the pitch of my voice and waved my arms around, saying "It's a symbolic number for completion, you know. It was used by the Hebrews, the Dutch, and the Village People. The number is often on our dollar bills."

Barb's was giggling by the time I finished my Janet Maples imitation. "You are so bad!"

I smiled. "The reason I'm here is to tell you that Jo called. They're four or five hours out. I invited them to dinner and told her I'd get them in some provisions. Looks like we're about to experience our first major winter storm tonight. They're saying ten to twelve inches and thirty-mile-an-hour winds."

I took back my iPad and checked the weather. "Whoa! Now it says up to eighteen inches! That's taller than Sojo!"

"Are you going out now? I'll go with you. We'll be lucky to find anything on the shelves. I imagine the natives have already stocked up."

"Yes, let's go. I'll get something to feed us all tonight, too. Oh, and don't let me forget. Jo wants me to turn the heat up. She's afraid Ellen will freeze."

"God knows, we sure don't want Ellen to get tense!"

The grocery store was not as bad as we imagined. We were able to get everything we wanted and deliver it to Jo's house with little trouble. After turning up the heat, I walked through the house to make sure everything was in order. It looked fine, although one thing did puzzle me: in her guest room, there were several black feathers on the floor. I thought I'd mention it to her when I saw her.

Jo called at 3:00. "Honey, I'm home! Thanks so much for warming the house and stocking the larder. Ellen was beginning to get nervous about being cold, and you know how that is."

"Oh, I do. I hope she settles down before dinner."

"Don't count on it. She's worried about the blizzard. We can stay here and fix something to eat. God knows, you provided us plenty to choose from."

"No deal. I have a stew in the crockpot and bread in the oven. And Barb made a cherry pie. Come on over whenever you want. We'll plan to eat around six. And bring Evan."

After dinner we chatted about our time in Plainview. Barb said that despite the stormy beginning, it was one of the most fun trips she'd ever taken.

Ellen replied, "I know you had trouble getting there but you did get to spend time with Mary Nell who's such a nice woman, so like her mother who was so good to me this past year letting me live in their apartment and work in the kennel for them then letting me go work for Josie when she left for here even though the holidays are over."

"Mmm," Barb replied.

"I thought the trip up here was so interesting driving though all those states I've never been to before from Illinois to Indiana to Ohio and New York then here where I never expected to be in my whole life." Ellen smiled as she took a breath. "Then getting here and seeing this house Josie's in is like a movie about the Revolutionary War or somewhere George Washington might have slept except I don't think it was built that early but maybe Abe Lincoln."

Jo's eyes widened. She looked mortified. "Well, yes. Are you ready to go home, Ellen, before it starts snowing?"

"I don't really know, Josie, if we would be safe enough there by ourselves after I saw the crow feathers in the floor of my room and you know crows mean death like they did for Shep but maybe we should stay with Ruth and Barb tonight for the duration of the storm so Evan will be safe and you too."

"You may certainly stay here," I interrupted quickly. "In fact, it would be fun to have a slumber party."

"I don't think I could slumber but knowing you are all here in the house with me and no crow feathers or fox fur is flying through the air would make me feel much more like trying to close my eyes so that I wake up to a snow-covered world like Vermont is supposed to look in winter but doesn't now."

"Crow feathers and fox fur? Ellen, what are you talking about?" Jo asked.

"When we first got to your house and you took Evan outside while I took my suitcase to the room at the front of the house you said was mine but it looked like it had been used for a fight since there were crow feathers on the floor and fox fur on the bed like it was pulled out but how did those animals get in your house and why were they fighting in my room and will they be back and for what?"

I jumped in. "Jo, I forgot to tell you. When I was at your place today, I took a walk-thru to make sure everything was OK, and I saw some black feathers on the floor of the guest room."

"Crow feathers are more indigo or deep purple than black although everyone always thinks they're black and even call them blackbirds but that's a different bird who got baked in a pie and nobody ever tried to bake a crow although sometimes people eat it."

Barb, with her chin propped on her hand, stared at Ellen for several seconds. "Um, Ellen, how do you know it was fox fur?"

"The ends are red but the roots are grayish brown just like any fox I ever saw in Oklahoma and I guess in Arkansas but I never saw a Vermont fox so I suppose it's possible that this was another animal but I don't know of anything else with fur of that particular color which I've liked ever since grandma let me play with her stole, don't you, Jo?"

Jo had that wide-eyed, stunned look of frightened animals. She merely nodded.

"OK, look, I think you should just stay here tonight, and tomorrow we will all go to your house and make sure there's no way animals can get in, although I don't see how they could," I said.

Barb nudged me and whispered, "Don't you start that."

Jo agreed. I think she just wanted some relief from Ellen's verbal assault.

Ellen was tired, too. She nearly nodded off while Barb described the visit from Sandy Pine Thomas. She yawned hugely."I'm good at puzzles and finding things and I want to look at everything you've found so far so I'll look for your treasure tomorrow but I think I have to go to sleep now if it's OK."

Jo and Ellen went up to bed, taking Evan with them. Barb sighed. "She's exhausting."

I agreed. "What do you make of the crow feathers and fox fur?"

"I am trying not to make anything of them. Maybe she hallucinates, too." She shrugged. "Jo must have told her about Colly and Abraham and the dream she had," she said uncertainly.

"I hope so. She's enough to deal with without being psychic." I said.

"You know, I kind of hope she is psychic. Maybe she can find the last treasure."

Chapter 33 — January 4

The Clorox man visited during the night. He'd bleached all color from the world. And softened all its edges into rounded pillows of white.

It had been a loud night. The wind howled; the dogs whined; I was up and down looking outside; Jo was up and down. When I finally got up for the last time, I felt battered. I needed coffee.

Downstairs in the kitchen, Ellen was up, dressed, and drinking coffee. She looked up and smiled. "It's beautiful outside," she said softly.

I followed her glance to the window. The backyard was spectacular. Eight or nine inches of snow covered everything. Drifts in places looked to be two feet deep. Bright splinters of light refracted everywhere the sun touched the snow while the blue shadows only served to enhance the brightness.

I hesitated to let Sojo outside. I wanted to see that unmarred surface for a few minutes more. Then I noticed that the birds had already been marking their paths with tiny forked prints. Small rodent prints, likely chipmunks', snaked from tree to tree. "OK, Sojo," I said, "go blaze your trail."

She dashed outside then stopped short as her chest rammed into a wall of snow. She stepped back, looked up at me, and then bounded forward, sounding her call, "Roo-roo-roo."

From upstairs, an echo sounded, "Roo-roo-roo." Evan was awake.

The two dogs looked as if they were jumping hurdles as they bounced through the yard. Soon very little pristine snow remained to sparkle its silent beauty. In its place was a trampled testament to canine joy.

I called the dogs in to feed them just as I heard the rattle of chains. "Oh, good," I announced. "The snowplow is here."

It took JR more than an hour to clear the drive and parking pad. Then he spent nearly another hour shoveling the sidewalks and a path for the dogs.

He knocked on the door to tell me he was finished, and I invited him in for a hot drink. He pulled off his boots and came into the kitchen in stocking feet.

Barb was dismayed. "Would you like something else for your feet? I bet they're frozen," she said.

"No, thanks. These wool socks have foot-warmer holders. My feet are toasty."

I introduced JR to Jo. "She's a new neighbor. She's renting the Abraham Crowe house around the corner," I told him. "But she's probably going to buy it, then she'll need your services."

JR nodded to Jo. "I already do that house. In fact, I just finished it. You're good to go."

"That's great!" Jo said. "I'm happy to meet you. What do you do when it's not snowing?"

"Mow and blow," he said. "That's me, Snow, Mow and Blow. Leaves, that is." He blushed.

Jo cocked an eyebrow, "I never thought you meant anything else."

JR blushed again. "Thanks for the hot drink, Ruth. Gotta be off. More snow to move around." He nodded to Jo, tipped his hat toward Ellen and Barb, and departed, whistling "Let it Snow."

"He's cheerful," Ellen noted.

"He always is," Barb replied.

"He has the strangest billing system. He bills far in arrears. I got a bill last week for mowing he did in June and July. But he seems to know what he's doing."

Jo pursed her lips, said, "Uh," then paused. "Uh, is he married?"

Barb said, "I don't think so. No ring."

"Interesting," Jo mused.

"See there," I said with a grin, "another incentive to move here!"

Ellen asked Barb if the treasures she'd found in the house were still in the living room. "I'd like to study them," she said.

Barb nodded. "Go ahead. I'm going to get together a brunch casserole and some fruit. I'm getting hungry."

Ellen exited to the living room as Barb went to her kitchen to cook breakfast. Jo and I sat still, nursing a new cup of coffee.

"So you think JR's cute, huh?" I teased Jo.

"No, not cute, precisely, but interesting. I like his ponytail. And it's unusual to find someone so cheerful. Hell, he's probably on heavy anti-depressants."

"No, I don't think so. We've chatted about his health theories. He thinks our health is primarily the result of what we eat and how we live. He said we need to eat local, eat fresh, and eat variety. And we need to live with minimal stress. I agree with him."

"Hmm. Not a bacon and potato guy, huh?"

"Oh, he probably eats both, but not to the exclusion of other things. Variety, remember?

Jo shook her head, "I'm being foolish. But he is an interesting guy. Not your run-of-the-mill redneck."

I looked at her over the top of my coffee mug. "Why haven't you remarried? I know you had a crappy experience with marriage, but that was many years ago. No interest in trying again? Or just nobody you wanted to try it with?"

Jo took a deep breath. "Do you remember Red James? Long, tall, lean cowboy? Lived out past Edith, about fifteen miles?"

"I think so. The funny one who came in for coffee every morning?"

Jo nodded. "He and I saw each other pretty steadily for about fifteen years."

"What?" I sloshed my coffee in my lap. "Really? My God, you were discreet!"

"Had to be. He's married." She said into her chest.

"Ah! And it's over now?" I asked softly.

"Yeah. His wife died, and he broke it off with me."

"Whoa. That's cold."

"I thought so for a while, then I realized it was the nicest thing he ever did for me. It made me take a hard look at my life."

"Thus the new persona?" I asked.

She nodded. "I decided I was tired of playing the unattractive, unthreatening Aunt Bea character I had used to divert suspicion. It was time I figured out who Josephine Murphy was."

"New clothes, new hair, new name, now new home. You don't do things by halves, do you?"

Jo laughed. "It needed doing." She looked at me carefully. "What about you? You never married. No big relationships?"

I gulped. "Remember when we were in high school? You and all the other girls spent most of your days dreaming about the boys with pimply faces and tight butts. I never did."

I thought for a minute. "Once, when I was in China this enterprising and very charming young woman asked me why I wasn't buying presents for my children. I told her, 'No children.' 'So why you no buy for your husband?' she asked. I told her, 'No husband.' She looked me over and said, 'You no like men?' I told her, no, that wasn't the case. I liked men fine. She examined me again and said, 'Ah! Maybe they no like you.' I laughed and bought whatever it was she was selling, but that exchange stayed with me. It was true. Men didn't like me. But it was also true that I didn't really like them either."

Jo nodded slightly. She reached across the table and patted my hand. Barb walked in carrying a tray and yelling, "Soup's on!"

I squeezed Jo's hand and shrugged. She went to find Ellen.

"Did Ellen leave?" Jo called from the living room.

"I don't think so," I answered. "I thought she was looking at treasures." Just then the doorbell rang.

Jo answered the door to a cold and wet Ellen. "What have you been doing? You're freezing cold!" she scolded.

Ellen's cheeks were rosy from the cold, but the sparkle in her eye had nothing to do with temperature. "I figured it out," she said. "I know where the other treasure is. If you get in your right mind, you'll know, too."

No amount of prodding, threatening, or begging would get Ellen to reveal what she had discovered.

"God," Barb said after Jo, Ellen, and Evan left for their house. "Can you believe we spent all that time trying to get Ellen to talk?"

Chapter 34 — January 5

The weather had warmed into the high twenties. Not warm enough to melt the snow except where it had been shoveled, but warm enough to make being outside enjoyable.

After breakfast, Barb, Sojo, and I walked to Jo's place to see if they had discovered anything about the crow feathers and fox fur, if that indeed was what they were.

Ellen greeted us at the door. "Isn't this a lovely day?" She raised her arms into the air. "I know it's cold, but it feels luscious! Now I understand how people can live here during the winter. Days like these make it bearable."

Barb's eyebrows rose as she glanced at me. I winked. I knew what she was thinking: Ellen *can* make a sensible statement.

Inside, Jo was seated at the dining table, engrossed in a large book. It looked ancient with its embossed leather cover and gold-edged pages. She looked up as we entered, holding the book up for inspection. "I found this on the floor in the guest room. It must have fallen from a shelf next to the bed. I knew there were old books stacked there, but I hadn't examined them yet."

She lay the book down and rubbed her eyes. "Look what I found among the pages." She held up a couple of black feathers and a strip of reddish fur. "I found the source, I think."

"Well, I'll be damned!" Barb exclaimed. "What's the book and why did it fall off the shelf?"

Jo shook her head slightly and rubbed her forehead. "The title of the book is *Communing with Loved Ones on the Other Side*. It was written by Abraham Crowe."

"Well, I'll be damned!" Barb repeated. "May I see it?"

Jo nodded. "It's heavy. Pull up a chair next to mine."

Barb and I complied, sitting on either side of Jo and straining to see the pages as she turned them. About a quarter of the way into the book, I spotted another small black feather inserted next to the binding.

"Is there anything important about these pages?" I asked. "Is the feather a bookmark or did a crow just fly over it, scattering feathers?"

Barb threw me her *look*. "Let me read this side." After a few moments, she said, "It's about Abraham's first encounter with his spiritual guide. I wonder…." She flipped to the front of the volume, to the Table of Contents. "Look," she pointed, "here's the beginning of the section on Abraham. Big section. And he wrote about himself in third person." She huffed. "OK, Colly starts at page 147. Is there a strip of fur at page 147, Jo?"

Jo turned the fragile pages carefully until she reached 147, and there, inserted next to the binding, was a thin strip of red fur. She leaned back against her chair with a sigh. "I'm glad you two showed up. I wasn't looking for patterns. Now I wonder if fur and feathers mark every reference to Abraham and Colly."

Barb turned back to the Table of Contents and wrote down every section devoted to either of the Crowes. She read the page numbers to Jo, who turned the pages.

When they finished, Jo said, "They're not at every spot, but then, some of them fell out. I think they must have been intended to mark each spot. But why?"

Ellen had joined us during the search. She asked, "Are each of those references to spiritual experiences of Colly or Abraham?"

Barb startled. She still wasn't used to Ellen's ability to speak cogently.

Jo answered Ellen seriously, "Yes, they are."

"Then the fur and feathers are important to the experiences. Maybe they are gifts to the totems."

Jo pursed her lips as she considered Ellen's explanation. "Barb, you told us about the symbolism of the crow. It's often seen as a harbinger of death. What about the fox? Other than slyness or craftiness, does it signify anything else?"

Barb pulled out her smart phone and tapped the keys for a minute. "Listen to this: the Chinese see the fox as being associated with the afterlife. When you see a fox, you are receiving a signal from the spirit world. And in Native American lore, a fox is seen as both a wise and noble messenger and as a trickster, luring people to their deaths."

Jo asked seriously, "Then are we supposed to see these fox and crow messages as connecting us to spirits or leading us to death?"

Ellen replied, "They're not malignant. They're just conduits. They are bringing you messages. Look for the connections."

"I'm sorry, Ellen, but I don't see any connection other than the fox sent me Evan for protection."

"You didn't tell me that, Josie!" Ellen blurted. "The fox is protecting you from the crow not the other way around. I had it backwards. Now, I see."

"And you see what?" Jo demanded. "I don't see a damned thing."

"Settle down, Sis. It's good. It's all good! You need to buy this house. You're going to live in it for a very long time."

Jo slumped in her chair. "Ellen, you are exasperating!"

"I know. But I don't mean to be."

Jo sighed heavily. "I know that, too. Maybe that's enough to know."

"Not quite," Ellen said quietly. "You also need to know that you won't be living here alone. And I don't mean Evan or me. Evan will be here for some years; I won't; but someone else will live here, too."

"Oh, God, not a ghost," Jo wailed.

"No, silly. A person. A man. Alive."

"See there, Jo. Now you've got something to look forward to," I teased. "Is there room to park a snowplow in your driveway?"

Barb and I chuckled. After a bit, Jo joined us.

Ellen, who was looking through the book, said "Laughter is good. It seals the promise."

"I have no idea what you're talking about, Ellen," Jo said, "but if I can laugh, live in this house with Evan, and even find a compatible man at some point, I'm happy to believe you."

"Ellen," I asked seriously, "how do you know all this?"

"I can't explain it, Ruth. I just get in my right mind, look to the light, and then I just know."

I left it at that.

As we walked home, Barb remarked, "I'm not sure Ellen has a right mind."

"She probably left it somewhere," I replied.

"That's bad," Barb groaned.

I nodded. It's hard to be clever when you've just been bombarded by a crow, a fox, and a loon.

Later that evening, Jo called. "I just wanted to tell you that I've decided to believe Ellen. I'm going to follow Coleridge's advice and willingly suspend my disbelief. I will have poetic faith in the supernatural and enjoy the gifts bestowed by the gods. Or at least by the gods of black feathers and red fur."

"I think that's wise, Jo. That sister of yours is not to be ignored."

"Amazing, isn't it. Oh, she said to give you a message. She said you need to look to the light."

"Well, that's helpful," I muttered.

Chapter 35 — January 6

The Twelfth Day of Christmas. The Coming of the Magi.
Epiphany.
A sudden illuminating realization.

I had a restless night. Ellen's words kept coming back to me: get in my right mind and look to the light. It sounded like hocus-pocus, but something about it niggled at me.

I tried to remember everything I knew about the treasure we had not yet found. All I could come up with was that it was under the old porch, whichever one that was.

I got up early. I tried to write in my journal. I managed about a dozen words. The sun still wasn't up, but the moonlight reflecting on the snow made it brighter than I could have believed. I stared out the window and thought about being in my right mind. Did Ellen mean being sane, accessing the right side of my brain, or tilting my head to the right?

I meandered into the living room and stood looking out the front window where I could see the sun had begun its inexorable rise. I tilted my head to try to see under the arched trim board covering the top of the porch's posts. I wanted to enjoy more of the bands of pale gold and peach that widely striped the sky. With my head tilted to the right, I noticed a beam of light that seemed to come through that board near the top of the arch.

"How odd," I said aloud. Sojo bumped her nose into my palm. I absently smoothed the fur on the top of her head as I studied the beam of light.

Suddenly, I had an idea. I walked outside onto the porch to see what the light beam illuminated. From the edge of the porch facing the house, I could see that the shaft of light was focused on a carved section above the door.

I stepped off the porch and took a few backward steps on the sidewalk, trying to find the hole that allowed that beam passage. I finally spotted it. Near the top of the right arch, was a small circle. It appeared to be made of glass. Or maybe a marble.

By then I was freezing in nothing but my nightgown and robe. I hurried back inside, trying to remember what I knew about lenses and focusing light. I dressed warmly and quickly, and hurried back to the porch with a step ladder in tow.

I climbed to the top step, holding on to the doorframe, and looked toward the origin of the beam. There was, indeed, some sort of globe or lens inside the small hole in the board. It was no wonder I had missed it before. It was only about a half-inch in diameter. If I had seen it, I probably would have thought it the home of a carpenter bee.

Satisfied, I gingerly turned to face the house so I could examine the illuminated carving. It appeared to have small hinges on the left edge, and a knob of sorts was hidden on the right between the ridges that edged the central motif, a raised pyramid.

I tugged on the knob, and the carved section pulled out from its surroundings. I tugged again, and it edged open a bit further. A third tug, one I put my weight into, nearly toppled me off the ladder. I grabbed at the doorframe to steady myself, and a section of the upper frame depressed. At the same time, the carved door, for that was indeed what it was, sprung open. Standing on tiptoe, I could see there was something inside the recess.

I shoved my gloved hand inside and felt around until I found what felt like a block of about four inches square and three inches tall. I pulled it out and held it to the light. "Of course," I muttered, "another damned tobacco tin."

I closed the carved door, climbed off the ladder, took it and the tobacco tin with me and went inside. I was cold and so excited I could barely get my gloves off. And my cold fingers wouldn't work properly. I couldn't get the lid off.

Just then I heard Barb in her kitchen. For some reason, I decided not to show her my discovery yet. I hid it in a drawer, put the ladder in the breezeway, and went into the backyard with Sojo, pulling on my gloves again as I went.

After a few minutes of Frisbee, I saw Barb gesturing to me from her kitchen window. I waved and threw the Frisbee again for Sojo. She was doubly delighted with this morning's playtime. She got to play with her Frisbee and bound through the snow at the same time.

Barb knocked on her window and gestured for me to come in. I complied. She had hot coffee ready. And although we chatted while we drank our coffee, I didn't mention my find.

It was only after a second cup of coffee that I was able to escape from Barb. It took several minutes for me to impatiently pry the lid of the tobacco tin loose and extract the envelope with a letter inside. The ink on the letter had faded to a light brown, the paper was fragile, and the spiky writing was difficult to decipher.

I decided I would transcribe the letter and give it to Barb as a fait accompli. I pulled out pad and paper, turned on the overhead light, and sat down to the task, when the phone rang.

When I answered it, Jo asked cheerily if I had eaten breakfast. "No, I haven't," I replied. "I got sidetracked."

"Good," she said. "Grab Barb and come over." She hung up before I could reply.

I hid the tobacco tin and the letter as I called to Barb. Then I started swaddling myself in layers of wool and down for the third time since I woke up.

Jo answered the door to two hungry, cold women and a very excited dog. Sojo loved to visit Evan. Ellen waved as she walked up the stairs. She'd already eaten, Jo told us. "Good," I said, "more for us."

We ate our fill, then lingered over coffee and discussed everything from the price of fuel oil to the impossibility of peace in the Middle East.

When Barb left for the bathroom, Jo poked me. "What are you hiding?" she whispered.

"Why do you think I'm hiding something?" I asked with some indignation.

"Ruth, you do *not* have a poker face. You look like the cat who's licking her whiskers after a canary lunch."

"Well, damn! Barb will probably know, too." I sighed. "OK, I'll tell you but don't say anything to Barb. I want it to be a surprise."

Jo nodded agreement.

"I found the last treasure. Your crazy sister was right. I had to look to the light." I heard Barb open the door to the bathroom. "I'll tell you later," I said quietly.

Barb sat down and looked at me carefully. She took a deep breath then looked away. She knew something was up, but she wasn't going to ask.

After we got home, I spent about an hour transcribing the letter. I had come up with a plan for showing it to Barb. I would turn it into my final Centerbury Tale. I typed, edited, and formatted it and inserted it as the twelfth tale.

I leaned back in my chair with a sigh of satisfaction when another thought intruded. Barb was likely to view this as yet another example of my hiding things from her.

Damn, I couldn't un-find the box.

I reached down to smooth the soft hair on Sojo's ears, a habit I had developed for times when I needed to think. I suddenly clearly heard Ellen's voice saying, "Get in your right mind and tell her what you're hiding." I didn't think she meant just the letter.

All afternoon I stewed. I thought first "yes" then "no." I thought maybe I would write a letter. Then I thought that was a coward's way. I'd have to talk to her. But how should I broach it? I nearly drove myself crazy with my what-ifs and if-onlys. Ellen was right. I needed to get in my right mind. I certainly felt out of it after all my waffling.

I tried to meditate, but the crawl-line of my circular thought moved faster and faster until I abandoned the attempt and began to pace. Sojo followed me from the kitchen to the dining room to the living room and back to the kitchen. She must have thought it a new game. But after about a dozen circuits, even she wearied of it. She ran in front of me and jumped up to lick my cheek.

I dropped to the floor beside her and hugged her to me. "I won't scare you off, will I?" She looked up at me and snuggled her head under my chin. I held on to her, rubbed her soft ears, told her what I was afraid of – disapproval, abandonment, friendlessness.

When I finished whispering in her ear, she stood up, found a ball in her toy box, dropped it in my lap, and said, "Roo-roo-roo." I knew exactly what she meant. "Just get on with it."

As I threw the ball into a snow bank, I suddenly knew exactly what to do. I'd show Barb my picture book and tell her how I came to make it. What a simple solution!

I cleaned myself up – I was covered in Sojo's hair – retrieved my picture book, printed a fresh copy of the Centerbury Tales with its new final tale, and knocked on the connector doorway as I entered Barb's dining room.

"In here," she called from the living room. When Sojo and I walked in, she looked up from her book. "What have you two been doing all afternoon?"

"I've been getting in my right mind," I said with a slight smile.

She tilted her head and raised her eyebrow.

"Just an Ellenism," I said with a wave of my hand. "I brought something I want to show you. Come sit by me on the couch."

Barb shrugged then complied. My book was lying face down on my lap. I turned it over so she could see the photograph that made up the front cover.

"I made this book from photographs I took, over about thirty years. It was a gift." I pointed to the woman standing next to me in the photo. "For Lily."

Barb looked at me carefully, then back at the book. "You're so young here."

"I was twenty-seven. Lily was thirty. We worked for the same company but in different offices. We met at a company picnic, playing softball. She pitched. I caught."

I flipped open the cover to the first inside page. Lily and I and the rest of the softball team covered the bottom half of the page. At the top, in large script, was the heading "And so it began...."

I flipped the pages, commenting on where the photos were taken – Bangkok, Bangor, Des Moines, Beijing, Tampa, Tokyo. We'd been to all of them and many others during the thirty years we worked and played and lived together.

I turned to the back page. It was another photo of the two of us, posed as we were in the cover shot. Be we were older, grayer. I was fatter, but Lily was skeletal. Bald.

Barb caught her breath and looked at me with tears welling in her eyes.

I closed the book, smoothed the cover with my hand, and said softly, "Breast cancer. I lost her four years ago. About six months before Janie called and asked me to move to Plainview with her. I had retired early to spend what time we had left with Lily. There was nothing else holding me in Chicago."

Barb reached for my hand. "I'm so sorry, Ruth. I know how it feels to lose a partner."

I took a ragged breath. "I know you do." I blew out the breath I felt like I had been holding for years. "You don't seem surprised."

"Oh, honey, I knew about you before you did, I think. I knew your heart was never with those boys you dated. You only lit up around certain young women. Mostly tennis players." She smiled.

"What tennis players?"

"Oh, Amy Buck. And Jessie Nance. And that cute little freckled redhead. What was her name?"

"Rosy," I said. "Rosy O'Malley. Yeah, she was cute."

Barb chuckled. "You were so transparent. You really shouldn't ever play poker."

"You're the second person who's told me that today."

"Oh, no! I'm not talking like Ellen, am I?"

"No," I laughed. "Jo."

"Well that's OK, then. She's usually right."

"You both are," I said quietly.

"What's that on the floor?" Barb pointed to the stapled stack of paper I had put there earlier."

I retrieved it and handed it to her. "I finished my Centerbury Tales. I want you to read them. I found my twelfth tale today, although I guess it's kind of a cheat. I only edited it.

"What does that mean?" She flipped through the pages.

"Read it," I said, "then I'll tell you about it. And about anything else you want to know."

Barb looked up at me for a moment. She looked down at Sojo and a grin twitched her lips. "That'll do," she said.

Centerbury Tales

Ruth Welborne

The Roommate's Tale

I bet you wonder why I'm calling at this hour of the morning. I waited as long as I could. I've been awake all night thinking and planning and making lists.

Yes, I still make lists.

I'm not sure how to begin. OK. As you know, I retired from my 35-year teaching job two weeks before Ben died. Everything I had planned for this part of my life died with him.

Now don't "Oh, Barb!" me. I am not being melodramatic. I'm trying to be realistic. We had planned to travel. He was going to retire next summer and we were going to get an RV and see the country. Actually, it was mostly his dream. I wanted to travel, but an RV sounds like too much work. I like hotels where my beds are made for me and restaurants where I don't have to cook.

Anyway, I am not going to buy an RV and head out cross-country by myself. In fact, I don't want to travel like that at all.

But staying here in this house we've lived in for 33 years is not a good option either.

No, Ruthie, I'm not afraid to be alone. But I hate being half of a couple. Almost all our friends are couples, and I just don't fit any more. And most of my women friends were from the school where I don't work anymore.

So I got to thinking about when I was last just my own person. You know, not half a couple. And do you know when that was? When we were in college.

No, my life hasn't been bad. In fact, there was a lot good about it. But after you're part of a couple for so many years, you forget how to be single. I don't know how to shop for one or how to cook for one or how to do much of anything. And it's mostly my own fault.

Ben took care of me. He handled all the bills, the taxes, the bank accounts. After he died, I didn't even know where the checkbook was. He paid everything online. He didn't write checks. I had no need to.

I don't want to be helpless. I want to be like I used to be. Remember how you used to say I was the strongest person you ever knew? I'm not that person anymore.

I have been trying to figure out how to get back to the in-dependent woman I once was. And I keep ending up at the same place – the time we lived together.

Now wait. Before you get scared, I am not looking for a Ben-replacement. What I want is someone who knew me the way I used to be who can help me remember.

No, please, Ruthie. Hear me out.

What I have come up with is a vision for the way I want to spend the rest of my life. I see friends of mine moving off to retirement centers where they plan to hang out until they die.

I don't want to go somewhere to die. I want to go some-where to live. I want to move somewhere I've never lived be-fore and have a big adventure. I want to wake up each morning excited about the possibilities of the day. I want to meet new people and learn new things. I want to make my own decisions and manage my own affairs.

I have spent too many years being the dependable and predictable Mrs. Barbara King, English Teacher. I want to be unpredictable. Maybe I'll learn to draw. Or belly-dance.

But I am kind of chicken. I don't want to do all this with no support system. I have cousins in a couple of interesting places, one in Arizona and one in upstate New York. I think I'd like to move close to one of them, but not too close.

I want a roommate. Someone to share expenses and experiences with. Friends, but independent friends. Does that make sense?

Does it sound appealing? Because you are my pick. I want to be roomies again. And to start another new phase of our lives together again.

No. Don't say anything yet. Think about it and call me tomorrow.

In the meantime, I'll be making lists.

The Sweep's Tale

I can see from your faces you're surprised by my appear-ance. It's the scarf, isn't it? Huhh. I know. I know. You ex-pected to see someone taller than 4'10", didn't you, heh?

Well, I may be short, but I'm good at what I do. In fact, I do what I do because I'm short. Huhh.

OK, let me set your mind at ease then I'll get on with my inspection of your chimneys. OK with you, heh?

When I was about ten, I was climbing around like a mon-key. Up trees, on top of houses, anywhere high. One day I was on the roof of my house, looking down the chimney to see if any birds were in it, and I heard my dad talking to my brother. Mad like.

So , it being summer'n'all, I climbed on top of the chim-ney and stuck my head down it. I wanted to hear my brother get what for, you know, heh?

So I leaned in as far as I could, trying to hear my brother bawling, and I got overbalanced and fell down the chimney. Huhh. And I landed in the fireplace, upside down with my legs tangled up in the damper and the kettle hanger.

Dad nearly fell over when he saw me. Huhh. And I was screaming. My legs hurt bad. My back was rubbed raw from scraping the inside of the chimney all the way down two sto-ries. Long fall, heh?

So anyway, I went to the hospital. Both legs broke. Bad broke. And kind of mangled. Yeah, nasty, heh? Then after the legs healed, they quit growing. Doctor said something about growth plates. Made me think about giant saucers. Huhh.

Anyway, by the time I was fourteen even I knew I wasn't going to get any taller. My arms grew though. Like a monkey, heh? That's why people call me "Chip".

Well, there's really a couple reasons. Before I fell, folks called me Chip since my name's Alvin. You know, them chipmunks, heh? Then afterwards, some called me Chimp, for the arms, but that never really stuck. Most everybody calls me Chip. Huhh.

So anyway, when I got out of high school, my dad told me I needed to find a job where being short was good. An advantage. And I thought and thought. It's not easy to come up with anything like what to do with your life when you're a dumb kid.

So anyway, one day I heard my little sister listening to her favorite video, Mary Poppins. And Dick Van Dyke was singing "Chim Chim Charee." And it hit me! I thought, "That damn chimney! It got me here. It can get me out." Huhh. So I learned to be a chimney sweep.

It wasn't easy, you know, heh? I had to talk a master sweep into taking me on. But when he saw me clambering around with my long arms and short legs, he was convinced.

Now here I am, Chip the Sweep. Huhh.

So show me to your chimneys and I'll do my stuff. No, I won't crawl inside today. I'll just drop my little flashlight camera down. That way I can see what's going on. Wish I'd had that when I was ten! Huhh.

Don't worry. I'll let you know what I find. Then we'll see about making sure you got a safe fireplace. Wouldn't want you to burn down your house. Or break your legs. Huhh.

The Jeweler's Tale

You like that pendant? It's one of my favorites. It's just a stone I found and polished, not valuable, but I like the striations.

Yes, it looks like the shape of a woman to me, too. It's $85.00. The setting is sterling. You can put it on a chain or a collar or a pin like this one; it's $45.00.

OK. I'll box them for you. Oh, for your niece. Do you want me to wrap it? I have all-occasion and birthday paper. Navy or red?

Hmm? Oh, I've had this shop about two years. I was born near here, at a commune up in the mountains. My mother's an independent sort. I'm not sure who my father is. I'm not sure she knows, either. Whatever.

Mom moved up to the mountains in the mid-seventies with a bunch of college kids getting back to the land. Whatever. I think they nearly froze and starved to death at first. Very little money, heated their shacks and tents with wood they cut, ate what they grew, found, caught, or killed.

When Mom got pregnant she decided she wanted a doctor to check her out. She got a lot of grief from the natural-birth bunch at the commune, but she didn't care. The doc agreed to trade checkups and delivery for a quilt Mom made. Ohio Star, I think.

Anyway, we stayed on the mountain until I was five when Mom decided I needed to go to school. Traumatic for me. I went from being nearly feral to having to wear actual clothing and shoes. And stay indoors for hours at a time. I'm still happier outside.

But at least we moved to Brattleboro. Lots of free spirits there. Mom would have shriveled somewhere more conventional. So would I.

I was about twelve when I decided to change my name. Mom named me Jodhpur Greensleeves. Really. I don't know why, really. Her story changed often, but it had something to do with what she was wearing either when she got pregnant or found out she was. Whatever.

Mom was a big Kris Kristofferson fan. Played his Silver-Tongued Devil album constantly. My favorite was "Jodie and the Kid." I decided I'd become Jodie Greene. I thought I'd fit in better at school. Mom said whatever. She didn't really care. It didn't really work, either.

I kept Jodie Greene through college. Then I kind of went over the same edge Mom had and moved to Sonoma. Arizona, you know. Fell in love with a Navajo, a jeweler. He taught me to work in silver. He was all into vision quests and ancestral stuff. Said he'd dreamed me before we met. Saw my face in a golden stone he'd found on his quest. Whatever.

Anyway, he convinced me to change my name to Gold Stone. I got kind of famous for my golden stone pendants. Made good money for a few years.

When that was over, I moved back here and bought this shop. Changed my name again. Jodie Goldstone. I think it's my best name yet.

Here's your package. I tied a little gold stone—it's just paint—into the bow. Hope your niece likes it.

The Historian's Tale

I was so happy to meet Barb this afternoon and discover that she lived in a Josiah Lake house. I've been dying to get inside one ever since I discovered the connection.

I've decided to take the two of you into my confidence. Don't worry. I won't tell you anything dangerous. Only what you need to know. To understand.

So. What do you know about Sacred Geometry? Squaring the circle? As I thought. No one pays attention to the Golden Section anymore. But see it in your mantle? This side rectangle is ten inches by sixteen inches. Phi. The Golden Section. Draw a square. Halve it. The ratio of the diagonal of the half to the original side is Phi. The Fibonacci series. Start with zero and one. Add them together to make the third number. Add the second and third to get the fourth, the third and fourth to get the fifth: 0, 1, 2, 3, 5, 8. Keep going. At any point divide one number by its predecessor. You get Phi. The Golden Section. Draw squares with the dimension of each number in the series and get a chambered nautilus. Do you see?

This house embodies the truths of the universe. One house begets two. A DUAL living house. Duality is implicit in all creation.

I see no explicit triangles, for the creative trinity, but the triangles are implicit in the beveled edges of the window frames.

And the pyramids! Oh, it is better than I imagined. The square with triangular faces. Diagonals rising up in praise of the One. The Golden Ratio!

Do you understand? This house is built upon the universal truths of Freemasonry, Necromancy, Alchemy, and the symbols of the Rosicrucians. We could conjure here. Maybe even contact George Washington. He was a Freemason. Most of the founding fathers were. Their symbols are on our dollar bills. And in your mantle.

I can see you are missing vital information. I apologize. I jumped into this too quickly. I was too excited by what I saw.

Let me start again. I am an historian, it is true. But I am also the seventh daughter of a seventh daughter. You don't see, do you?

Very well. Maybe you don't need to know. Perhaps I expect too much. I've spent years moving from one truth to another. I can find no one else who understands the importance of my work, except one very old professor at Princeton. She knows.

Oh, well. I continue to try. I must. Or when I leave this body all the connections I've discovered will be lost to time. And it's much too late for that.

One last attempt. Let no one say I didn't try.

Sit down, please. Listen with your inner ears. Discount your doubts and hear my truths.

I have discovered that all the universal truths of life can be expressed in the Sacred Geometry used by the Master Builders of the Pharaohs. The same proportions, ratios, arcs and chords were repeated through the centuries by other master builders and passed down to their apprentices. Until they made their way into your house.

I was challenged to find this truth by my maternal grandmother, one of the hidden Abenaki who descended from the first inhabitants of this land. Her truth expressed itself in

Abenaki terms. She sent me out to find a way to express those universal truths in European terms.

I believe I have.

But she also told me I must not forget my Abenaki roots. Despite eugenics. Despite the forced sterilizations and attempts to annihilate us, we have survived. Hidden. Blending into European society. But we must seek ways to teach our truths even now.

Do you see? Your house sits in a sacred site. Abenaki sacred. Josiah Lake knew the Abenaki and the Europeans. He built their truths into these walls.

His secrets must be unlocked.

I will help you find the key.

The Plumber's Tale

Stay there. I can find my way to the light switch.

I was in a jungle so dark you could see a match lit four or five klicks away.

Yeah. Viet Nam.

I was there 'til I got bayoneted. See this scar above my shoulder? Went clear through and out the back of my neck. Hit an aorta. Squirted blood everywhere. Lucky I was near a MASH unit.

Nice cellar. We can run the pipe right here. See? These two pipes come out of there, and we can connect them here. The tank will be here, next to the drain. I can do the electrical too. I'm a master electrician.

Got my training at Fort Knox. Down in Kentucky. A linesman. Worked on big stuff. One night a big fucking thunderstorm was going on. My buddies and me were drinking beer and playing poker at the NCO club – I was a sergeant – when we got called out for a downed line.

Now, they got reset poles – stick 'em up and reset the transformer. Back then, we had to climb the poles. So there we were, soaking wet and climbing poles. My buddy says, "What the fuck kind of idiots are we? Playing with electricity in the fucking rain?" Just then a big clap of thunder boomed and I damn near crapped my pants.

See here? The line from the toilet comes down here into a trap and on to the main sewer. Trap keeps sewer gas out of the house. Damn. This old stuff. Can't do traps like this any-more. They get filled up with human shit. Have to be cleaned out. But they work.

Anyway, we told our CO we wanted to do something else. We didn't care what. Just sick of electricity. He sent us to Ft. Benning, in Georgia. Special forces training. That kicked our butts!

What kind of idiot put that line in like that? See how this boot is attached to that old iron pipe? Idiot should have taken out that whole length. Bust it off here and there. Put in new. Never leak again. Damn fool jack-offs, call themselves plumb-ers.

Next thing I know I'm in a jungle. My friends getting killed. One of 'em shot middle of his forehead. He lit a ciga-rette. Damn fool! He knew better. He KNEW better. I'm still pissed off at him.

Another buddy fell in one of them holes covered over with branches and shit. Sharp bamboo sticking up inside. He hol-lered and hollered. Begged me to shoot him.

I dreamed about him for years. Heard him yelling. Won-dered did I do the right thing. My wife had to sit on top of me to keep me from...flailing around.

They sent me to Hawaii to recover. "Battle fatigue" they called it. Gave me drugs. Put me on a metal table and shocked the shit out of me. Hundreds of times. Fucking electricity.

There's room in the box for a double-pole breaker, 30 amp, if we move this circuit. I can do that. Easy. Get the breakers at Home Depot. Just Square D. Nothin' special.

I'm 63. I could retire. Get military pension and social se-curity. But I don't want their fucking money. I'm considered disabled. That bayonet? It paralyzed my left arm. It was dead. And I couldn't turn my head.

When I was in Hawaii, I met this woman. Japanese. Went to live with her in Japan for a while. Her uncle was into martial *arts. He took these little needles and put them all the way up my arm, from my little finger to the back of my neck. Couple rows of them. Every day. Two, three times a day. For weeks. After a while, my fingers started to tingle. Just a little. I thought at first I was imagining it.*

Then I got more tingles in my hand and arm. Pretty soon I could move a little, then more and more. He taught me martial arts to strengthen my arm. Still do some of those exercises. They worked.

Look here. See that back-facing faucet? That's to drain your outside spigot. You gotta do that before it freezes or you'll have a mess. Frozen pipes sometimes thaw without breaking. But not very often. Most times you'll be calling me to come fix 'em when it's colder than shit outside.

I came back here and got a job. Learned to be a plumber. Been doing it 30 years now. Almost half my life.

One day I got a special delivery package. A Purple Heart, a Gold Star. And papers to fill out for disability pension.

No, not "Wow!" It pissed me off. I packed them all back up in the box and mailed them back to Washington. A few weeks later, MPs show up. Took me to Washington. Asked me why I sent back the medals and papers. So I told 'em.

I told 'em about being in the jungle, too dark to see shit, when we saw a glow 3 or 4 klicks away. My buddy and me, we belly-crawled to the top of ridge where we could see with our night binoculars what was going on.

There was a string of lights, about half-covered up by a tarp. And our officers and a bunch of others were loading barrels of heroin into boats. Stamping them to take back to the States.

Worse thing I ever saw. Worse than the bamboo spikes.

They said it wasn't a "war." It was a "police action." Police are supposed to keep things safe.
Fuck!
Wish I couldn't see so good in the dark.
I'll turn out the lights.

The Handler's Tale

I never expected to be living the way I am. Sixty-six years old, single, raising two teenagers.

Yes. My grandkids. Boys. Charlie's 15 and Denny's 13. My daughter named them after me, she said. Charlie for Charlene and Denny for Denise, my middle name. Makes it confusing now that they live with me full-time.

I've had them nearly two years. Since my daughter got sent to jail. Oh, I know it's not an unusual story, but I never thought it would be mine.

Kim, my daughter, was a great kid. Pretty, bright, funny. Good in school. The perfect kid. Until her dad left. She was about Charlie's age, 13.

Such a tough time we had. I was scared and angry. Angry at Bill for leaving me for some 20-year-old chippy. Scared because I hadn't worked since before Kim was born, and I was petrified I wouldn't be able to find a good enough job to keep us alive.

Oh, Bill said he'd support Kim. And I guess if you call "support" the odd twenty-dollar-bill given out of guilt, then he did. What a jackass he was! He'd set up "dates" with Kim then not show up. She had gone from being Daddy's little princess to Daddy's afterthought. The only attention she could rely on from him was lectures when she acted out.

So act out she did! In spades! Boys, sex, drugs, alcohol, theft, pregnancy, abortion. She tried it all. Bill screamed at her. She did as she pleased.

By the time she was 16, she'd been picked up by the cops twice, thrown in the drunk tank, and bailed out by Bill. He was such a help.

I got therapy for myself. I had no notion how to handle her. Luckily I found someone good. She taught me about enabling and sent me to Al-Anon. That saved my sanity. I learned how to let go and let God, and pray every day that Kim survived.

I kept busy. I had a good job, traveled. I had friends. I worried about Kim, but over time the pain eased.

Then Kim got tangled up with a Mexican drug runner in Arizona. I don't think I ever knew how she got to Arizona. But she played house with Pablo for a while. Until he was deported and jailed in Mexico. That scared her.

About eleven years ago, a dirty, skinny, strung out woman hugely pregnant and carrying a little boy appeared at my house. I didn't recognize her at first. I hadn't seen her in several years, and those years had not been kind to her.

She shoved the baby in my arms and wrapped me in a hug. She said woodenly, "Oh, Mom! I am so happy to see you. This is your grandson, Charlie. Can we stay with you until I get on my feet?"

I was pole-axed. A grandson! And I was pissed. Showing up like that after all that time. I kept Kim standing on the porch while I sorted myself out. I took a deep breath and let her come in.

I told her she could stay a month. Then I looked at her enormous belly and asked when she was due.

"In a month," she said softly. If she had been brash or snotty, I would have sent her on her way. But that soft reply got me.

"OK," I said. "You've got three months. That's all. You'll have to find a job and somewhere to live after the baby's born."

And she did. She had an easy birth. Named the baby boy, Denny, after me she said, and found a job waiting tables. She got a little apartment, found daycare for the boys, and started going to AA.

I held my breath, waiting for her to fall. But she didn't. She kept going. She got stronger. I thought I had my daughter back when she disappeared.

One day she was there. The next she wasn't. And I didn't see her or hear from her for more than ten years.

It was while she was gone that I got involved with agility. I needed something to get me out, give me exercise, keep me from obsessing. I was getting old enough to retire soon. I knew too many people who retired into depression, feeling that they'd lost their identities with their jobs. I didn't want that.

I've known Ann a long time. She suggested I get a dog and train for agility. I finally gave in to her steady urging and got a rescue border collie who needed me as much as I needed her. She was terrified of life. She hadn't been abused, just neglected by a well-meaning but incapable owner.

Long story short, Matilda and I became a team. We ate together, slept together, played together, ran together, surprisingly won together. She's got a string of titles a mile long. But like everyone, she got old, arthritic, and not as excited about running as she once was. I had slacked off, running rarely, when Ann called again with another dog who needed me.

Ann came to my house with a beautiful Aussie girl, Mickey, whose owners had to move to a place that wouldn't allow dogs. I knew Mattie's running days were over and I couldn't imagine not having a dog to run with. So Mickey moved in, in-

gratiating herself with both me and Mattie. That was a little more than two years ago.

We had just started training in earnest when Kim showed up again with 13-year-old Charlie, tall, tan, and timid, and hyperactive Denny just turned 11.

Kim told me she had to find a safe place for the boys. Their father was out of jail and was determined to find his sons. Would I keep them safe?

I told her I had to think about it. She could stay a week while I figured things out. I was 64. I had retired two years before. I loved my life. Could I do it? Could I take my grandsons, two very needy, scared kids? Could I not?

I never prayed harder. I saw a lawyer. I went to every Al-Anon meeting I could find. I talked to everyone who would listen. I made lists of pro's and con's. It finally came down to my own sense of morality. Could I live with myself if I didn't take the boys?

At the end of the week, I told Kim that the boys could live with me but she couldn't. I wanted her to grant me guardianship so I could enroll them in school and get them medical care when they needed it. And I demanded that she NOT reappear and whisk them off to God knows where again. She would see them only during supervised visits.

She cried. She begged. She said she'd changed. I let her cry and beg. But I didn't back down. I don't even know how I had the strength to get through it. But I did. And she left.

I've heard from her twice in two years. Once she was in Mexico, drunk. The other time, oh, I don't know where she was but she was coherent enough to talk to the boys for a long time. I think that was a mistake. They were upset for days. It hurts them. But she is their mother. I just don't know what's right.

Not surprisingly, the boys have lots of issues. They can be combative, teary, apathetic, defiant, depressed, and clingy.

Sometimes all within the same day. I've got them seeing a therapist, and I guess it's helping. Sometimes it's hard to tell.

But my agility friends have been wonderful. They've helped me with the boys, given them jobs cleaning kennels and walking dogs. Luckily, both of the boys love animals.

I hate to think how I would have made it without the help of my friends. They've even made it possible for me and Mickey to enter a trial now and then by finding constructive things for the boys to do. It's such a treat to be able to have a day to myself when I can concentrate on nothing harder than directing Mickey to the right tunnel in the right order.

See my bumper sticker? I believe that: "Dog is God spelled backwards."

The Contractor's Tale

I can't believe they way they "fixed" that wall. Covered up the rot with new boards. Oh, yeah. They knew what they were doing. Just hiding the problem. Trying to sell the house.

You should have called me to look it over before you bought it. I do that. People call me. Oh, well. Next time. None of this is too bad. All of it can be fixed. Don't panic.

We only have to pull off the claps, replace the sill, sister new studs to the old ones, put in a jack to support the roof while we're working. Then re-sheath and re-side it.

I know it looks scary and stuff, but it can be fixed.

Most everything can. That's what I love about my job. I can fix beautiful old buildings, make them look better than new. Or as good, anyway. Just takes time.

I know about fixing things. See my leg? The scars? I tore it off in a car wreck. I was nineteen.

No, it's OK now. It's shorter than the other one, but I don't even limp. Just a few scars and stuff.

I was in the hospital two years. The bones healed, but I got infections and stuff. The skin grafts wouldn't hold. I took so many antibiotics, every bug I had got resistant. They kept opening up my leg – seven times – finally left it open to heal and washed it out 5 times a day, and stuff. Kept grafting skin from my other leg. See here. And here.

Oh, yeah. I took a lot of morphine. Had to. Amazing pain.

The worst was when they took a long strip off my good leg and grafted it onto this one while it was still attached. Oh, yeah. Then they had to elevate it to keep down the fluid buildup. And my legs had to be totally still. They screwed them together. Oh, yeah. And hung me upside down for six weeks. Talk about a headache!

When they took me down, I couldn't move either leg. Atrophied. After the skin graft totally healed I had tons of therapy. Months. So I could move again. And walk and stuff.

The nurses were my family. I mean, my own family came to visit , but I was there two years. Nobody should have to give up their life for two years. My mother took it hard. It was better when she didn't come.

Anyway, when I finally got out, I was institutionalized. I don't mean I had to be put in an institution, but maybe I should have been. I was addicted to being in an institution, to the noise and never being by myself, and the nurses and stuff. Oh, yeah. I was addicted to it. And to morphine.

I couldn't function out of the hospital. I had lots of therapy and stuff. Most guys wouldn't have made it. Given up.

But I kept at it. I got better. I learned most anything can be fixed. Oh, yeah.

Don't worry about the wall. We'll take care of it.

The Painter's Tale

Do youse like this flat white? Oh, yeah, youse probably have to use flat. It's more historical. I know how them historicals are about stuff like that. So just flat white, right?

Did youse know that down of the Cape they are historical, too, but they can paint other colors than white. I don't know why you'd be stuck with white. I mean, why don't youse go talk to the historicals in town about it? Maybe youse want a yellow house. Is it against the law? Youse should stick up for yourselfs. Youse know what I mean?

I mean I didn't stick up for myself and that's what got me in trouble. I wouldn't say "No." Not to my dad or my pals or my wife or the girlfriend. I don't think any of them ever heard the word come out my mouth. Youse know what I mean?

When my dad made me leave school and help out with the family did I tell him "No"? Hell, no, I didn't. I mean we did need the money. But shit. Making me leave school at 14! And wha'd he think I'd do? Get a job as a doctor? Youse know what I mean?

I got in with rough kids. They taught me how to make lots of money. Selling junk. To kids. I mean dope. Youse know what I mean? Then I got to taking it. Made me feel better 'bout not going to school. Not making nothin' of myself. Youse know what I mean?

I mean I had to keep sellin' more and more to keep me in the shit. Then I sold to a cop. Twice. I mean, stupid kid! Eight-

een years old making tons of money and pumping most of it in my veins. Horse. Youse know what I mean? And sold to a cop! Shit!

Anyway, I got out after seven years. Upstate. I was clean. Ready to start over. Youse know what I mean? And my wife wants to leave. Take the kids. I let her. Didn't say "No." Shit.

Hang on. I'll move this ladder. Just a minute. I gotta take these pills. For my blood. Youse know what I mean?

So then I get a girlfriend. She starts using. I was still clean. But I didn't say "No" to her neither. She left after her mom died. All she did was ride my ass anyway. Youse know what I mean?

I mean, shit! Even my sister and brother-in-law are sick of me. He got me this job. And I'm good at it. I mean I like paint-ing. Especially white. It covers all the rot and bad shit up. It's like snow. I mean real snow. It covers up all the shit and makes it look pretty. Youse know what I mean?

I mean, shit! Your house'll look good. Youse know what I mean?

The Neighbor's Tale

You know, we came to Vermont to get married. And stayed. Two things I never expected: Vermont and getting married. Oh, honey!

I didn't intend to marry Jack. Or anyone else, for that matter. My first marriage was such a disaster. Oh, my dear, you can't imagine. I squired her around. I could pass then. Still can. I thought that was all she wanted. But no, my dear, she was a nympho. I admit I was a pretty hot property then, but eeeew! I hate to think about it. I did get her pregnant. Twice. It should have been enough. But not with Janice Hot Pants. Oh, I shudder thinking about it.

She was pretty, in a Barbie-doll way. About as many brains, too. But her daddy had money. Lots. And her daddy was a friend of my daddy. You thought arranged marriages only happened in India and China? Oh, my dear!

It lasted eight years. God knows how. The kids were seven and five when I left. I loved those kids. I should have taken them with me. That was a big mistake! But she caught me in a delicate position, if you get my drift. And she told her daddy who threatened to tell my daddy if I didn't leave town. He didn't want his grandkids to be influenced by me. But honey, half their genes were mine. How much more influence could I be?

I was still afraid of my daddy. When I was thirteen, he'd promised to kill me if he ever caught me with another man. I believed him. But Mamma understood. Protected me from Daddy.

I don't know why I let him rule my life for all those years. He was a mean bastard. And I was scared-kid fragile despite my brawny good looks. Best thing I ever did was leave that town. Except for the kids. I loved those kids.

Oh, they're both in their late thirties now. We're pretty close. Sue has three girls. Cute? Oh, honey, they are adorable. And Tony has a son, Andy. Just out of high school. Troubled. He doesn't set off the gaydar. I think he's probably straight.

I'd like to help Andy. Ah, we'll see. Jack's a little hesitant. Said he wasn't cut out to be a step-mother and he's too young to be a fairy godmother.

Did I tell you we're going to take the girls to Disneyland in February? I made arrangements for them to have lunch with the Princesses. They will love it.

And honey, I'll love it. I always wanted to be a Princess.

The Artist's Tale

In art school, everyone was such a purist. If you were going to paint the figure, you had to do it from life, nude. Well you didn't have to be nude, but your model did. If you were going to paint a landscape, you had to do it outside. Those French Impressionists made it impossible to feel good about painting in your studio. They said it wasn't true if you didn't paint from the direct image.

But I wonder. When you are outside, the light changes every minute. Which minute is true? Isn't there maybe more truth in painting your own experience of the scene, frozen in time, in your own imagination?

I feel perfectly fine about taking photos and using them for a studio painting. Not that I want to copy a photograph, but it is my reference. Or one of them. My most important reference is the memory of my reaction to the scene.

At least nowadays, I can paint what I want. And I love to paint the Vermont landscape. The sky is never the same. The mountains change color with the light. And subject matter? The forest, the barns, the cows and sheep, the steepled churches, the brooks and rivers. All of it there for the taking.

When I come back to Centerbury, I have even more to work through in my painting since I have so much emotional content already connected to this place. I grew up here. I look at that stream and remember skinny dipping in it. Or parking and necking with my first boyfriend at the top of that hill. Everything is loaded with my prior experience of it.

Maybe that's why my best paintings are those I paint here. They are much harder for me. But after I struggle through them, I think I sometimes find what's really true.

And it's not because I painted them outside.

The Snow-Ploughman's Tale

I've been doing this for about six years. I like it. I'm my own boss. People need me. I'm useful. What's not to like?

Well, sure, the cold. But it's not bad. Most of the time I'm in my truck. It's warm. When I do have to hand-shovel, I can work up a sweat and stay warm. You just have to know how to dress. Layers. It's all about layers. Put 'em on and take 'em off. Don't get too hot, don't get too cold. That's all there is to it.

Oh, sometimes we have a warm winter with not much snow, but not often. And if we do, I can find something else to occupy me. And I mow grass in the summer. That always needs doing. And I clean up leaves and clean out gutters in the fall. I do OK.

I don't make loads of money, but I don't need it. I've figured out how to stretch my income throughout the year. My house is paid for. I make enough each season to maintain my equipment. What else do I need?

My parents do not understand why I'm living this way. They spent a ton of money sending me to good schools. I've got an MBA in Finance from Wharton. I had a high-power, high-earning, high-stress job at Bear Stearns. I made tons of money. I lost my wife, my kids, and damn-near my life. A heart attack at age 38.

So I started looking for something else to do. Somewhere else to live. Somehow to live with less stress. A friend let me *stay in his camp near Winhall. And I fell in love. With the place, the pace, the space, the people.*

Then I knew where and how I wanted to live. I just had to figure out what to do. And that only took one big snowfall.

I think I have the best job in the country. Just look at that beautiful snow.

The Joiner's Tale

This house was a gift I built for my wife. I spent seven years laboring on it, like Jacob trying to earn the right to marry Sarah.

My Sophia was worth the all my labor and more. We were so happy in this house, we thought ourselves uniquely blessed. Our daughters were testament to our joy.

Those twenty-five years with Sophia were heaven on earth until the final year, when I lost all of them within three months. First Mary, then Anne, and a month later, Sophia. She hadn't the heart to keep living once her daughters were gone.

I struggled with the deep sorrow that engulfed me. For five years I remained in my house, seeing Sophia or one of my daughters around every corner. I was no longer alive, but my body refused to comply with my deepest wish to join them. I was unable to take up my tools. I mainly sat and rocked and berated the God who took my happiness from me.

When I began to fear that I would succumb to the lure of death, I left Centerbury. I wandered for four years from New York City, to California and back. Once by sea; once by land.

As I traveled I began to regain my life. Once, on the gold fields in California, it came to me that I was enjoying myself. I was happy to wake in the morning and see before me a day in which gold might come to me. And I began to pray again.

A short time after this revelation, I encountered an old prospector. We conversed for some time when he told me something that has never left me.

"You may look at me and think me a fool. I have been seeking gold for several years. I have found some, barely enough to keep me. I am not a rich man except in experience.

"I have, however, gained understanding of gold. I know this: having gold does not make you happy. It is a worry: someone might steal it from you; you must guard it. Whatever you might think now, being constantly watchful and fearful will rob you of happiness, not grant it.

"No, having gold does not make you happy. Finding it does. Oh, that leap of joy when you spot the shine in your pan. Oh, the dreams it ignites. Everyone should have the opportunity to find gold."

It wasn't long after that meeting that I decided to go home again. I wanted to return to my work of building homes and churches and even barns. I wanted to be useful. And I wanted to delight someone.

For some time, I studied on how to accomplish that. How could I enable someone to find gold?

After much prayerful meditation it came to me that my house could be a goldfield. I could create an opportunity for someone who came after me to find gold, both actual and figurative.

And so I built a false wall beside fireplace, with a hidden latch to open the wall and expose a secret room. I placed items in boxes and secreted them in various locations around my house. I created clues that an avid seeker would find.

And you, dear reader, have found my gold. I pray you also found some measure of delight in it. If so, I beseech you to re-seed my goldfield for some future seeker. True delight must be shared to endure.

About the Author

Kathy Wagenknecht lives in Bennington, Vermont, in a dual living house with two border collies and a talented painter.
Visit her at her website: *kathywagenknecht.com.*